RETAINED

Book 2 in the Irrevocable Series

SAMANTHA JACOBEY

Lavish
Publishing LLC

First Edition

Book 2 of Irrevocable Series

All Rights Reserved

Published in the United States by Lavish Publishing, LLC, Midland, Texas

Cover Design by: OliviaProDesign

Cover Images: depositphotos.com

Paperback Edition

ISBN: 9780692440841

www.LavishPublishing.com

Contents

For my mother, Linda. Without her, much of this tale could not, or would not, have been written. Thank you for our family, which has taught me what crazy really means…

Prologue

PETER MASON AMBLED down the hall, waking the boys and preparing for their day. Glancing up the stairs, towards the third floor, his chest ached.

But, in the end, he knew he couldn't let it show. Making his way to the bathroom, he slogged through his routine and worked his way to the kitchen, where a pot of coffee awaited.

Taking his place at the table, the boys joined him, smiling and digging into the morning meal before them. Watching the pair, he ate a few bites of the delicious scrambled eggs, not enjoying them nearly enough. Folding his hands under his chin, he put his elbows on the table, still stuck in his funk while he stared at the empty place at their side.

Pete had been trapped between the needs of his community and those of his niece for a while. In the end, his attempt had been small, almost feeble, and probably not enough to save her. Of course, what he had done was enough to disrupt all their lives if anyone were to find out. *Just breathe,* he reminded himself. *You'll know how it worked out before the day is over.*

"Hey, guys." He leapt to his feet, his heart skipping a beat when Luis and Devon came through the door. Not hesitating for a moment, the two disappeared through the other passage, and he followed them onto the front porch. "I thought you were taking care of Bailey this morning," his voice dropped in agitation.

"We gotta problem," the shorter man gasped with hands on his hips.

"What kinda problem?" Pete shifted, already uneasy at their plans; having issues only made it worse.

"Da girl's gone," Devon supplied, leaning his tall frame against the railing. "All 'er stuff's still in 'er room, too."

"Yeah," Luis corroborated his story. "We scoured the entire compound, comin' up empty."

Peter stared at the pair, his jaw slightly hanging, and gasped, "You're kidding me. An' no one's seen her?"

"No one we talked to, no." Devon turned, hunching over the top rail and scanning the horizon through narrowed slits.

"Did you talk to Bill? Surely he doesn't think that I had anything to do with this!"

Luis shook his head slowly. "It wasn't you." Staring, he waited for the older man to make the connection.

"Caleb." Pete shook his honey and silver waves. "Son of a bitch!" He feigned surprise, careful to keep the grin from breaking through to the surface.

"So whadda we do?" Luis wrung his hands eagerly.

"We need a meeting right away. Gather all the *menfolk,* an' let's see if we can find out how long ago they left an' what we're gonna do about it." Slamming the screen door behind him, Peter knew he would be walking a thin line as the day unfolded.

He had put the bug in Caleb's ear the previous morning, filling him in on the community's decision about the girl's future.

Not sure if the young man would actually act on her behalf, he had tried not to worry about it, either way. Now that he had, Peter Mason wasn't sure if he was glad or annoyed that his best friend's son had run off with his niece, and he certainly hoped no one discovered his part in it.

ONE

Second Time Around

PULLING up outside the apartment just before four, the sky appeared pitch black. Killing the engine, Caleb fumbled around in the darkness to locate his key, indicating for his companion to follow. "Thank God I came t' stay with you guys before we left town," he mumbled to the groggy girl stumbling up the stairs beside him. "Otherwise, we'd be locked out."

"Yes," she agreed, leaning on the railing. "Mine's in my bag back in Lawson."

"You mean at The Ranch," he corrected.

"Wherever the hell it is." She pushed her way past him. "Man, I am dragging-ass tired."

"I know." He turned to lock the door behind him, while she disappeared down the hall. "Crash on the couch or should I take Pete's bed?"

"Pete's bed has no sheets," she called, flicking her own bedroom light back off. "None of them do, remember? We took them all with us." Making it back to the sectional, carrying a pillow, she took the short segment, with her head pointing at the door. Flopping down on it, she exhaled noisily. "This works. Goodnight."

Caleb grinned at her, lifting her foot and removing a shoe. Her eyes still closed, he wasn't sure she even noticed. Dropping it on the floor, he pulled the second off, then took care of his own. Lying so that their feet met in the curve of the couch, his head settled on Pete's arm rest. *Man, are we in trouble.*

His body ached from the overnight ride, but his mind had been racing since they had refueled, and he had passed the point of no return. *I couldn't let them do it,* he told himself for the umpteenth time. Closing his eyes, he breathed deeply, willing himself to sleep.

Awakening to the sound of his cellphone, Caleb sat straight up in the dimly lit room, only half aware he still lay in the same spot. Flicking the blinking screen open, he heard the voice of his father demanding loudly, "Where th' fuck are you?"

"Hi, Dad," he replied, coughing slightly.

"Don' *Hi Dad* me, you little bastard! Are you outta yur God damned mind?" the man ranted.

"No, I'm not. Please, jus' hear me out." The younger Cross rubbed at his eyes, allowing the phone to drift away from his head to check the time. The other end remained silent, which he took as consent to speak. "We're in Midland. You can tell th' rest o' them not t' worry. I got this covered. I'm gonna get my job back, an' Bailey's gonna finish school. An' then we'll be home. That's what you promised her, an' I'm holdin' you to it."

"You'll be home today! What th' hell were you thinkin', carryin' her off like that?"

"Dad, I only got one thing to say to you, an' then I'm gonna hang up. An' I know you're gonna understand, 'cause we don' want any trouble. We jus' wanna be left alone an' let her finish school. You understand?" Caleb waited again, ready to make his bluff. "Clayton Hill," he finished calmly.

The line dead silent, the young man watched her prone body taking shape in the hazy morning light. A full minute later, he could hear the sound of ragged breathing. "Dad?" he spoke more quietly.

"Are you threatenin' me?" the older Cross finally managed.

"No, Dad. I'd never do that. What I'm sayin' is you should let us be. Let me take care o' her, an' let her finish what she needs to here. Then I'll bring her home. I swear." He waited for a moment, but no other sound came over the connection. "Please, Dad, let us do this. Let me do this. You know I'm right about her."

"No, son, I don't," the other man spoke more calmly. "You an' I both know this's a community decision, an' they ain' gonna like it."

"Then don't tell the community where we are. Otherwise, then I might be forced to reveal certain things to certain people." He lay back down as he spoke. "An' no that ain' a threat. I jus' wanna be clear where we all stand in case there's trouble."

"Oh, there's already trouble," John Cross growled. "I'll see if I cain't buy you some time, son, but there ain't no guarantees."

Caleb chuckled into the device. "Nope. Never are. I'll call an' check in later. Let you know how things are goin'."

"You better'd," the older man challenged.

Running his fingers through his blond spikes, the young man's hand relaxed against his chest, still holding the device. Tapping the back cover with a nervous finger, he pondered their situation until he fell back to sleep.

Several hours later, Bailey rolled over, blinking into the light to discover Caleb stretched over the other end of the couch, breathing loudly. Spying the cellphone in his hand, she stood, quietly sliding it out of his grasp. Flicking the screen to open it, her heart began to pound, the name John Cross appearing at the top of the call log.

"Hey," Caleb's voice startled her as he reached for the phone.

"Your dad called you?" she panted, staring into his clear blue eyes.

"Yeah," he huffed, pulling himself up. "An' it's ok. He's gonna calm everybody down. We get t' stay here an' take care o' business, an' then we go from there."

"Uh-huh." The girl peered down at him with wide green eyes.

"Why do I find that hard to believe?"

He rolled his tongue for a moment, unsure of her demeanor. "Are you mad?"

"Mad? No. I have people wanting to kill me every day. Why should I be mad?" her voice rose steadily as she spoke. "Oh, because this is the second time you have lied to me... Yeah, that's why!"

"Lied to you?" He got to his feet. "I don't think I have ever lied to you, Bailey." He paused, considering his actions more closely. "Maybe I never tol' you everything, but I never lied," his tone became equally loud.

"For your information, leaving important shit out...is lying. But you grew up in the sticks, so there's no accounting for your screwed-up values," she hissed.

Towering over her, he took a step towards her. "An' here I thought you'd be grateful for me savin' your life."

"My life wouldn't have needed saving if you had been honest with me in the first place!" Turning on her heel, she stomped out of the room, slamming her door behind her. *Son of a bitch!* Moving over to the corner she had made her desperate call from a few short months ago, Bailey slid down the wall, facing the room.

I have no money, she pondered. *And I have no phone. Both of them are in BFE along with all my other must-have belongings.* Pushing her face into her hands, she willed herself not to cry. *I told you to stay away from him. Why didn't you listen?*

A few minutes later, Caleb came in to perch on the foot of her bare mattress, facing her. "Well, it looks like you an' I need t' talk."

"There's nothing to say," she pouted into her palms.

"Ok, then I'll talk, an' you listen." He folded his arms across his broad chest. "I realize there's a lot o' things I ain' told you. But they aren't things you need t' know." Her face shot up to glare at him as he continued, "I'm lookin' out for you, little bit. I know you don' see it that way...but I swear—"

"You were going to let them take me!" she cut him off with a quivering lip.

"Uh, no. I jus' hadn't figured out how I was gonna stop them." His clear blue orbs glared at her. "Trust me. If I thought you knowin' woulda helped, I woulda tol' you. Ok?" He inhaled deeply, pulling his eyes away and running his fingers through his hair.

"What we need t' do now," he continued more calmly, "is t' get ourselves together. We need sheets for the beds, we need food, an' we need a plan."

"They're coming, aren't they…?" her voice trailed away.

"No, they're not comin'. Like I said, my old man's gonna take care o' things, an' we'll be fine. We do what we gotta do here, an' then we go home."

"I'm not going back there." She shook her head slightly. "I was lucky to get away the first time. No way in hell am I going to give them another chance to finish me."

He nodded slowly, his head making more of a circle like a bobble-headed doll. "Ok." He met her glare for a moment, his distorted features stretched and exhausted. "Don't worry about th' stuff I don't tell you. I'm jus' keepin' it safe for you until you're ready to know it."

Standing, he offered her his hand, and she allowed him to pull her up. Squeezing by him, she moved to the lavatory to wash her face. Staring at herself in the mirror, she realized how odd her own face appeared, giving herself a grimace. Finished with her primping, she knew he was right, and the pair needed to stock up for their stay.

"Let's go to Wal-Mart," she suggested when they exited the apartment. "They have everything all at one location, so we won't be running all over town."

"Ok," he agreed. "But it'll be packed. It always is."

"I don't care," she retorted. "Let's just get it done." Stomping down the stairs, she pulled her hair into a ponytail and climbed onto the seat behind him.

Arriving out front of the supercenter a few minutes later, they made their way inside. Selecting a cart, they walked straight through to the linens that could be found on the back wall. "Pete's bed is a king," she supplied, looking through the bedding. "What pattern do you want?"

"Cheap," he replied crisply. "What they look like don' matter."

Finding a clearance set of sheets and a comforter, she dropped them into the basket. Choosing a twin set for herself, she frowned that they didn't match but tossed them in as well. Steering the cart, they followed the outer wall to the food end of the layout, picking up milk and butter spread, then eggs. Turning right at the corner, they selected lunch meats and cheeses.

Pushing into the section of meats, the crowd grew thicker, and Bailey had to wait before she could move any further. Standing still, she cast her eyes over the throng of people, her pulse becoming louder in her ears.

Her fingers tingling, she adjusted her grip on the blue plastic handle. Inhaling deeply, she pushed the air out through pursed lips; the sound of the people seemed to crush in around her, and for a moment she felt faint.

Moving in so that his chest brushed against her right shoulder, Caleb ran his hand down her spine, his fingers firmly making contact. "Relax, little bit. We got plenty o' time."

Growing stiff at his touch, she continued to breathe until a small path had cleared and she could move forward. Gathering a package of steaks and a larger tray of chicken breasts with trembling digits, she mumbled, "We need bags for dividing so we can freeze this in smaller sections."

"Good plan." He smiled at her choices. "I'll get 'em an' meet you at the end, by th' bread." He darted between the traffic jam and headed for the correct aisle.

Continuing alone, Bailey collected a variety of fruits and fresh vegetables, then swung around to find Caleb waiting for her, a whole wheat loaf in hand. The sight of it jolted her, and her gaze returned to her selections, her eyes slowly roving over the ears of fresh corn and bundle of carrots. "Wow, I didn't even realize—" A buggy crashed into her and interrupted her train of thought.

Dropping his collection of flour, sugar, bags, and bread into the basket, Caleb caught the corner and spun it around, steering it towards the check out. "Le's get outta here!"

"No argument from me," she agreed, fairly certain they had forgotten something but unwilling to remain in the cramped space any longer. Standing in line, they waited only semi-patiently, and a child in the seat ahead of them began to wail loudly.

Turning her back to the toddler, Bailey stood facing her roommate, her eyes boring into his Adam's apple, only inches from her nose. Hearing the loud hacking cough of an old woman in the line next to them, her eyes cut over to take in the smaller, hunched figure, her wrinkled palm only partially blocking the spasm. Shuffling ever so slightly closer to the man before her, she allowed her eyes to close.

Caleb raised his hand, laying it lightly on her hip, then applying firm pressure for reassurance. Lifting his chin, he rested it on the hairline above her forehead. He could feel the tension of her body, aware that the crowd around them had put her on edge. Holding his own respirations under control, he focused on her, telepathically encouraging her to remain calm.

A few minutes later, they moved to the counter and began placing their items on the conveyor. Pulling their bags off the other end, they pushed the cart out to the motorcycle, where they stuffed her comforter and all of the sheets into the left saddlebag. The food items went into the right, and he strapped his oversized blanket onto the back.

Wiggling into their seats, she clung to him on the ride home, grateful for the fresh air and sunshine that surrounded them. Her fingers laying against his broad chest and her right cheek pressed into his back, she could feel her pulse returning to normal. When they made the last turn, she smiled, suddenly aware of what they had forgotten—new makeup.

TWO

Fruits of Our Labor

CLIMBING THE STAIRS, their arms laden with parcels, the couple maintained a relaxed quiet, each of them relieved to be out of the crowded store. Opening the door, Caleb began to add to their list of chores. "We have t' get a few things done, but I guess some of it can wait 'til tomorrow."

"Yes," she agreed quietly, a little less bitter towards the man next to her. "We have to get our jobs back for one. Mine's easy though. I can walk over in a few minutes and take care of that." Her mind recalling the small shop next door to her employer, she continued, "And I can pick up another phone while I'm there if you wouldn't mind fronting me the money."

Caleb grinned, carrying his new bedding towards the back of the house and happy that she seemed to be over her fit of anger. "I can give you some," he called over his shoulder. "We're gonna need it, so the sooner you get it the better." Dropping his items on the floor, he opened his wallet to pull out two one hundred-dollar bills. He offered them to her when she came down the hall. "Is that enough?"

"Should be." She pinched them between an index finger and thumb. "I'll pay you back as soon as I get paid."

"No, you won't." He raised his chin as a challenge. "We're in this together, so it all comes out the same." Dropping the subject, he turned to put his bed together. "Go make us some dinner, an' I'll take care o' this part."

In silent agreement, Bailey returned to the small kitchen, dividing up the meats into a few smaller packages and placing all but two steaks into the freezer. Taking out pans, she prepared their meal, her mind returning to the small town in the middle of nowhere. *I hope the boys are ok.*

As soon as the beds were in order, Caleb returned to the front of the house, taking a chair at the table to watch. The evening sun filtering through cracks in the vertical blinds behind him, he admired the view of the kitchen. "Sure beats frozen lasagna, don't ya think?" he commented as she set his plate before him.

Only nodding, she took her seat. The food had turned out perfectly, bringing the slightest of smiles to her lips. "I guess there were a few good things that came out of my time at The Ranch."

"Oh yeah," he agreed. "I think it's better when we can appreciate the fruits of our labor. City folks don' really get t' do that, not like we do back home."

Not bothering to disagree, Bailey enjoyed her plate in silence, then stood to clear the table and load the dishwasher. Her task completed, she stated matter-of-factly, "I'll be back in a bit."

"I'm comin', too." Caleb sprang to join her. "I thought o' something else we need, an' there's a shop over in th' strip I can get it from."

Crossing the street together, he left her at her place of employment and made his way around the corner to the furniture store that faced the loop. Inside, he purchased a television, hauling the oversized box home to set it up on the cherrywood entertainment center, which occupied the front wall of the living room.

Meanwhile, Bailey felt relieved to find Mark heading up the

troops as usual. "Hey," she greeted him with a small smile. "I'm back. Think you might still have a place for me?"

"Of course." The shop manager grinned. "Come on, and we'll get you activated on the time clock."

Following him to the office, it only took a few minutes for them to complete the new forms and change her status in the computer. "I'll put you on the regular schedule starting Sunday." He grinned. "And you can come in at five every day until then, if you want. You need some new shirts?"

"Sure." She smiled, happy to have the spares. Leaving a few minutes later, she moved next door, where the clerk helped her pick up a new go-phone similar to the one she had before. Glaring down at the device, she pondered which Facebook account she would attach to it before shoving it in her pocket and exiting the store. *Those belonged to a girl I don't really know any more.*

Arriving back at the apartment, she glared at the giant box sitting outside the door. Stomping inside, she demanded, "What the hell is this?" Her hand flopped open to indicate the screen that he had been staring at while he flipped through the channels.

"It's…a…television," he quipped.

"And why do we need that?" she commented curtly, displeased that things were beginning to look so familiar.

"Relax. I didn' get a game or anything. Jus' the set. For news an' stuff." He chuckled. "You know, I think bein' at The Ranch changed you a lot."

Bailey scowled, angry at his observation. "It's late, and we have things to do tomorrow. I'm going to bed." Not waiting for a reply, she sauntered down the hall and closed the door behind her.

His eyes wide with surprise, he watched her fiery highlights as they disappeared from sight. *Late, huh? It's only nine o'clock.* Her sassy attitude brought a small smile to his lips, and he returned his attention to the flicker of the new set, continuing to scroll through until he had favorited a few more channels.

That task complete, he double-checked the door and made his way to his own room. Removing his clothing, he opted for a shower before he slid between the new sheets. Lying in the greyish darkness, he contemplated his trip to visit the cement plant in the morning to ask for his job back.

If they don't have a spot, I'll have to hit a few others. He knew it wouldn't be hard to find employment somewhere, as nearly everyone in town needed workers. *That's one nice thing about living in a boom town. Maybe the only nice thing.*

The following morning, Bailey awoke before the alarm. Making her way out to the kitchen, she opened the fridge and peered inside. Closing it, she tried the freezer, then a few of the cabinets. Restless and not ready to prepare her meal, she opted to go for a run. Donning shorts and a tank, she headed out the front door and jogged the block, only mildly afraid of running into Ked. *It's too early for a sloth like him to be out and about,* she reasoned. *And with Caleb's training, I might not be able to whoop him, but I could damn sure get his attention.*

Arriving back at the apartment a short time later, she slipped into the shower and dressed in more average clothing. Feeling more relaxed, she strolled into the kitchen for the second time to make their breakfast. Catching her by surprise while she scrambled eggs and browned toast, Caleb entered through the front door, covered in sweat.

Spying her through the narrow window, he grinned. "Do I have time for a shower?"

"Not if you plan on a hot meal," she teased. She wanted to be angry at him, but the friendly way he regarded her seemed to make it impossible to maintain. Placing their plates on the table, they enjoyed their meal in comfortable quiet.

"I'm headed over to the plant today, so I may not be home until late if they have a truck for me," he informed her when he had finished.

"All right." She cleared the table. "I go in at five, so if you're later than that, you'll have to find dinner."

"I'll jus' come over there, like always." He smiled that she thought of his needs. "I'm gonna register for another class, too. Since there's a computer in the boys' room, it should go a lot smoother this semester. When do your courses start?"

"Next week, I think." She loaded the washer, adding soap and cranking the dial. Sinking back into her chair, she prodded, "We're really ok here, right? I don't have to worry about someone appearing out of the shadows to grab me, do I?"

"Well, you always wanna be cautious." He smirked. "But no, there won' be anyone comin' t' get us from The Ranch. I'll call an' check in today like I promised. We'll stay in touch with what's goin' on out there, an' it'll go smoothly." His eyes darted over to the wide screen inside the wooden box, drawn to the broadcast of violence across the country.

"Why'd you buy that thing?" she queried, following his gaze.

"So we can follow what's happenin' in the news, same as we did at The Ranch. I set the auto-tune to a few news channels, in case you're interested in checkin' any of 'em out while I'm gone today."

Bailey stared at the device. She had never really been a big TV person, only watching the popular shows that her friends from school took an interest in. She had discovered the members of the community down south preferred much different programming, feeding on the doom and gloom that some networks thrived on. "Something's really going on in the world, isn't it? Something I couldn't see before."

"Naw." He ran fingers through his damp spikes. "Your eyes are open now, that's all. You see things differently." Hauling his tired limbs to his feet, he made for the hall and the shower beyond.

Returning to the kitchen, Bailey made sure everything was in order and planned her day. She had a little money left over from the phone purchase, and she would need to secure a new bus pass. *And I need to go to the credit union so I can get my debit card sorted out.* Yup, she had a full day ahead of her as well. *Lying on the couch watching the idiot maker will have to wait.*

Exiting their tiny haven at the same time, the couple went their separate ways, each tending to business. Arriving back at the house in time for lunch, she prepared a sandwich and made her way to the desk to use the computer. Bringing up her Mason profile first, she deleted it. Then opening the Dewitt version, she made the necessary changes for her new phone.

Leaning back in the chair, she stared at the screen, blinking slowly while her thoughts churned. Using the mouse, her lengthy list of friends blurred as she scrolled through it. Clicking another icon, she switched to the news feed, taking in the never-ending list of nonsense. *These guys are nuts,* she breathed through a clenched jaw.

Flipping back to the list of people, she began unfriending. What had taken her years to build only took her fifteen minutes to destroy. Coming to Louise Mason, she stared at the name, curling her tongue. Clicking the envelope, she crisply typed a message. *Hi Nanna, things are great! Here's my new number in case you want to reach me. How's everyone doing back home?* Hitting the send, she wondered how many days it would take for the older woman to notice and respond.

Staring at the single name that remained on her contacts, she typed a new one in the search bar. Locating the right Peter Mason, she sent the friend request. Then, going through every person by name, she added them all, starting with Caleb. When she came to John Cross, she hesitated, her hand beginning to tremble as it hung over the mouse. *What the hell are you doing?*

"I'm spying," she replied almost immediately, speaking to the empty room and the screen before her. Only half worried whether or not they would accept the requests, she managed to find a profile for everyone aged fifteen and older from the community. *I wonder why they're on Facebook.*

It seemed odd to her that a group of recluses would choose to use the social media. Of course, all of their pages were the highest level of private, the same as hers, so she wouldn't be able to tell anything until someone let her in. Cleaning off her timeline as well, she created a single post. Sitting back into the chair again, she smiled at the specialness of it, considering for a moment what it would be like if the group actually accepted her in their midst.

Noting the time, she shut down the device and made her way to her own room to get ready for work. Not having replenished her supply of makeup, the process went much quicker, and half an hour later she was at the light, ready to take on the droves who would be dining with her that night.

THREE

Friend or Foe?

PETER MASON STARED at the screen in disbelief. *Bailey Ann Dewitt has sent you a friend request,* he read the notice again. *Holy shit!* The hairs on his neck stood on end, and his thoughts raced. *Either she doesn't know what we had planned for her or she doesn't know that I was involved.*

Shaking his head, he clicked the small blue accept button, unable to resist the temptation to spy on her through the connection. A moment later, he could feel his pulse in his throat; her friends list had been annihilated. Only six people remained on it: his mother, himself, and four people from The Ranch. *What the fuck are you up to, Bailey?*

Her timeline had also been cleared and every post hidden or removed, save the latest one. He glared at the life event, which read, *Joined Lawson.*

That can't be! There could be no way for her to *join* Lawson. *First off, she has no clue what Lawson is.* He ran trembling fingers through salt and pepper curls. *And second, why would Caleb allow her to do this?* Clicking on the latter out of his list, he typed a message and hit send. Leaning back in the chair, he ran his digits around his mouth, formulating his next move.

Rising, he shut down the system and headed for the diner, where dinner would be waiting, along with a room full of potentially pissed off people. *They know,* he breathed, his steps quick. *They have to know. Four of them already accepted, and I'm sure she didn't stop there.*

Pushing on the glass door, he made his way through the line and gathered his meal, joining the boys at a table in the center of the room. The pair seemed oblivious to what was going on around them, while the noise level in the room dropped to half when he took his seat. Before he could even begin eating, the chair next to him became occupied.

"We need t' talk," Bill Tate huffed.

"Yeah, I know," Pete agreed. "Soon as dinner's over. Have Laura gather the boys an' take them over to the park for a bit so we can hold the meeting."

"Ai'ght," the other man agreed, vacating the seat and getting to work arranging the guest list and who would be taking care of what.

Thirty minutes later, some of the square tables had been pushed together in the center of the floor, with the *menfolk* seated facing one another across the newly expanded surface, seven in all. Their wives and the remainder of the male adults of their community sat in a ring of chairs, surrounding the group to listen to the discussion.

All of the sons and daughters had been dispersed. The younger members of the township had been assigned to an older caretaker, who would ensure bedtime rituals were followed in case things ran long with the elders.

Sitting up straight in his chair, James Fox cleared his throat. Glaring at John and Peter equally, he considered which of them he should yell at first. "You realize this's a fine mess th' two o' you's put us in." He didn't mince words, laying the blame equally between them.

"Yes, I realize this." Pete leaned forward, laying his arms onto the laminate in front of him. "But throwing fits an' pointin' fingers isn't gonna help us."

"Agreed," John joined in, stabbing the surface with an extended digit. "That girl's got my boy's head all screwed up—"

"That girl?" his best friend cut in. "That girl hadn't done anything until your boy went to runnin' his mouth about things that shoulda been kept secret!"

"That's enough!" their patriarch interceded. "We're all well aware o' who gets th' blame here." He glowered at the two before him. "What we need t' figure out is what t' do 'bout it."

"Well, I promised Caleb we would leave 'em alone, which is what you all agreed t' do yesterday." John exhaled loudly. "An' I still think that's a good plan. O' course that was 'fore she went 'n clumped us all onto her Facebook an' put Lawson all across th' front of it."

"You noticed that, too, huh?" Pete dropped his voice, addressing the man to his left.

"You bet yur ass I did." He winced. "She's got some seta balls."

"She don't know what Lawson is, John," Pete countered. "She's smart. If she knew what it was, she wouldn't have done it. I think we been handling her all wrong, an' it's time we put a little faith in her," he raised his voice as he went.

"I have to agree," Chris Burns spoke up. "I realize this's highly sensitive info she's got out there, but she got it from somewhere...or someone. An' she don' know all the facts. This could be her way o' askin' to be let in. I'm thinkin' she's settled down, ready to be a part of us."

"To do what?" Bill clomped the table with a closed fist. "First off, women don' sit at the table. They know what we wants them to know." Several of the surrounding circle began to fidget. "An' they're a damn sight more respectful than that girl's ever been."

"You've known her for a month." Pete opened his palms in surrender. "The month after both her parents died, at that, so you know she's in pain. Her world changed at the drop of a hat, an' you can't tell me any of you wouldn't have acted out in a similar circumstance."

His face grew tired, his own sorrow exposed. "An' in that month, she became a whole 'nother person, meeting the challenge we laid before her. I think John's right. We should back off an' give them a little time. See what she does. Send her a quiet message to pull down the Lawson reference an' see if she'll fall in line."

"An' what if she don'?" the angry man held firm.

"If she don't, then we'll go from there." Peter shifted uncomfortably. "You know, I was real sorry I even had to bring her here. If my mother woulda taken her, or if I felt like I coulda left her there all alone, I would have." The man's eyes grew wide as he pled for his niece. "But it didn' work out that way. If somethin' had happened to her, it woulda been on me. She's *my* flesh an' blood after all, not some piece o' trash I found on the street."

No one had a fast retort to his latest bit of sentiment, and Pete looked around the group, his voice overflowing with conviction. "So she came, an' she got a taste for life on The Ranch. A whole different way for her. Le's see what she does with it before we do anything stupid. If not for her...then do it for me. I think I've earned at least that much here."

"That's right," John quickly backed him up. "After all, we know where they are, an' my boy'll keep tabs on 'er. Plus, they're upstate now. Not so easy t' get to them without drawin' attention, an' we all know the las' thing we want's attention." John cut his eyes around at the group that surrounded him, narrowing them into accusatory slits.

"An' Caleb knows way more about this place than she does. I hate to say he'd turn." He waggled a finger in the air. "He was raised here after all. This's his home. But you know how it is when a man's dippin' his wick."

A small mixture of groans cascaded around the room.

"You can't tell me he's not," his father continued. "You all seen the way they was together." He cut his glare over at his best friend. "If we push him, he could really hurt us with what he knows," the ex-marine finished, alluding to his son's threat. "An' for her, he jus' might do that."

An extended silence fell over the group, with more of the women and men in the outside circle beginning to whisper. Finally, Connie stood up. "I have sumthin' to say…if you don' mind hearin' it."

"Come on then," her mate proffered his approval of her advice.

"I watched that girl from the time she came t' the time she left." The oldest woman stepped closer to the tables. "I knowed who she was the mornin' she first set at my table." She paused for dramatic effect. "An' I seen who she was 'fore she left. We got a lot to lose here, but no more than she does." She cast her gaze on her uncle. "You wanna send her a message, you make it clear. Them boys's still here, an' if she were t' put anything out there, it might become necessary for them t' disappear."

"Agreed," he replied softly to her request. "I'll let her know. Until then, I say we all friend her an' follow what's going on the best we can. Le's make her feel welcome and let her see what she's missing by not bein' here, same as we did before. We do, after all, want her to come back."

"Does that mean you want us to include her?" Alissa also stood, considering the budding relationship the two had shared. "I think we were friends. We might be able to persuade her rather than force her hand."

"By all means," James agreed, shooting a glance at a few of the others. "My wife's takin' a hard line, but we do want 'er back here even if we have to wait." He nodded at his youngest daughter. "I know several o' you got closer to her when she was a part o' the community. Give 'er things t' think about. Reasons t' see our path… an' to choose it."

Listening to her father with a small nod, Alissa's eyes darted around the small group. She had felt connected to the girl the few months she had been inside their walls, and in the end, she knew

Bailey really didn't have a choice. *And neither do I. These guys are gonna get their way, with or without my help.*

Stopping by the apartment, Caleb had a shower and changed into more comfortable clothing, borrowing from Pete's closet. Combing through his hair, he thought about the tall auburn-haired girl he would be seeing in a few minutes. *Well, not as tall as 'Manda, but almost.* He grinned at the comparison, realizing full well that Bailey suited him far better of the two, at least in his eyes. *And what anyone else thinks don't really matter.*

Flicking on the computer while he slipped on his shoes, he wanted to check his inbox and message his father. Clicking on the icon, he watched the program open to Bailey's page, and his heart leapt into his throat. *Oh shit!* Not even bothering to shut down the system, he exited the room and bolted for the front door.

Pulling his phone out, his profile popped up, and he accepted her friend request. Then he navigated to her page, the post jumping around, glaring at him as he stomped down the front walk. Leaving the screen up, he headed across the street at near a dead run. Inside the store, he stood in line, calming his breathing while clenching his fists as he waited.

Presenting himself before her a few minutes later, Bailey could see the panic in his eyes. "Are you ok?"

"No!" he practically screamed. "Tell your boss we have to go—right now!" Spinning around, he pushed through the line and marched to the door to wait for her.

Dumbfounded, she followed his command, making an excuse and retrieving her purse. "I'm so sorry, Mark. I have no idea what's happened!" she offered for the second time on her way back by.

"No worries, Bailey." He took over her register. "See you tomorrow, if you're able."

When she joined Caleb, they exited the restaurant, but he didn't give her a chance to speak. Pulling out his phone, he lit up the screen. "What the fuck is this, Bailey?!?"

She stared down at the timeline, her lips drawn into a heavy frown. Her green orbs cut up at him, she gave him a wide-eyed stare, not lifting her trembling chin. "It's just a post. I thought it would help."

"HELP?" he shouted. "No, it ain't gonna help." He ran fingers through his damp spikes, turning away from her. Becoming aware that they were still surrounded by tables, chairs, and people out on the patio of her store, he groaned. "Le's go." He squeezed her arm, guiding her towards the light.

"I don't understand!" she stammered, following his lead.

"I know you don't." His tone softened when they reached the other side. "You have t' take it down an' hope that no one from The Ranch saw it."

Bailey's blood turned to ice in her veins. "But they already saw it!" She recalled the moment of joy on her break when she had seen her friends list filled with twenty-two new names. She stopped moving, and he swung around to face her as she continued. "I sent them friend requests, and they accepted!"

His eyes glared into hers for a moment, faltering slightly as he searched them. "They friended you?" he breathed.

"Yes. All of them. Even Amanda," her voice quavered slightly.

"Shit," he swore under his breath. "Come on. Le's go find out if they're comin' t' kill us." Grasping her hand, he held her firmly, guiding her up the stairs and into their living room.

Locking the door behind them, the couple moved to the bedroom, where her profile still displayed on the screen. Caleb taking the chair, Bailey hunkered on the edge of the bare mattress next to him, watching as he clicked on the red message alert.

Bailey-girl, you gotta take that down, right now, please.

Her uncle's words gave her chills.

Two clicks later, the post had been removed. Sitting back in the chair, Caleb traced his lips with his fingers, pulling roughly at them for a moment and staring at the warm glow before him.

"I'm really sorry, Caleb. I thought"—she sucked in loudly—"I thought this was what you wanted."

Shifting his eyes over, he considered her apology. "I'm really hungry, little bit. Would you mind makin' me some grub?" His grin appeared strained, and she quickly agreed, leaving him to head to the kitchen.

As soon as she left, he opened a second browser from the desktop and accessed his own account. There he found a message from his father, stating that they had held a *meeting* and basically informing him that they needed to straighten up and fly right, or more innocent parties could become involved.

Caleb could feel the blood drain from his face, leaving him ghost white an instant before an angry flush took its place. "How dare they!" He slammed a closed fist onto the wooden surface, loud enough it gave Bailey a start in the other room.

"Are you ok in there?" she called, her hands hanging over her mixture and covered in flour.

"Yeah," he shouted back, putting his fingers on the keys. *Call me*, he typed, and hit send. Not thirty seconds later, his phone began to chime.

Making it to the balcony before he accepted it, "How dare you!" he spat into the device.

"How dare I?" his old man countered. "I tol' you yesterday this was a community matter!"

"Yeah, I got that, but that ain't no reason t' go threatnin' those boys! They ain't done nothin' t' deserve it, an' you damn well know it!"

"I know it, an' you know it, but that ain' gonna stop anyone from hurtin' them if it becomes necessary. What you need t' do is get a handle on that red-headed bitch o' yurs."

"Ok, just stop right there 'cause I know where this's goin', an' I got news for you. I DON'T OWN HER!" He looked around, aware that others might hear him, and dropped his voice. "An' on top o' that, I got more respect for her than that. Now, I know we need t' deal with this, but I swear t' you I will handle it. I will make her understand how important this is, an' she won't do it again. Ok?"

John listened to Caleb breathe for a long moment before he yielded. "Yeah, I think we're clear then. You take care of it, son. I'll talk t' you in a day or two."

FOUR

Random

DARKENING THE DEVICE, Caleb leaned his head against the support pole. Reaching up with his free hand, he steadied himself for a moment and gathered his thoughts, breathing in a slow, deep pant. When he felt calmer, he made his way over to the door and entered to find the girl still moving about in the kitchen.

"You ok?" he asked quietly, making his way around the large sectional sofa and into the dining area.

"Yes." She nodded, turning to place his plate of chicken-fried steak and mashed potatoes before him. "Are you ok?"

"I'm fine. You made all this?" His eyes grew wide, dipping a finger in the gravy and sucking it loudly.

"Of course," she exhaled the words, smiling meekly. Giving him a small shrug, she plunked down in the chair across from him. "So, what did they say?"

"They said"—he grabbed his napkin, then switched to knife and fork to begin dismantling the meal—"that they're pissed."

"Ok, they're pissed. What are they going to do about it?" Her lip formed a small pout.

"Well"—he shoveled in a few bites, letting her dangle in suspense —"we have to straighten up, which means I need to explain a few things to you."

"Some of that stuff you were keeping safe for me," she predicted.

"Yeah," he agreed. "Some o' that."

Sitting back, she blew out loudly through her nose. "All right, eat your dinner, and we'll talk when you're done."

Standing, she moved over to the kitchen and began cleaning the pans and other cooking utensils before loading them in the dishwasher. Wiping down the stove, she glanced over periodically. Eventually, she noted that he had cleared the plate and had begun removing the remnants of creamy sauce with a slice of bread. Grinning at him, she exclaimed, "Wow, you really were hungry!"

"Oh, yeah," he grunted. "An' that was delicious!"

She smiled from ear to ear, surprised that he would pay her such a compliment. "Thanks." Taking the plate, she finished up with the tidying and started the washer while he explained his news.

"First, I need t' tell you this isn't your fault. I should never have said the word Lawson t' you. You should've never heard it, an' I'm sorry." He stared at her, his blue orbs pleading forgiveness.

Taking her seat, she nodded. "Ok, I get that. So why is it such a secret?"

His eyes glazed for a moment. "I can't tell you that part. All I can tell you is you shouldn't ever mention it again."

"You don't trust me to know?"

"It's not for me to decide." He blinked rapidly. "An' you don't jus' walk into town and decide to be a member. Everyone there's part o' the family."

"Not everyone," she corrected, thinking of the four unattached males of the group. "You still have those random guys there."

He shrugged. "They're still part of us. They were invited t' be there."

"Why?" she clipped the word, causing him to lean back and study her for a long moment.

"Be…cause…they have military training an' other skills an' beliefs that make them good candidates for our community."

"Survivalists," she supplied the word coolly.

"Yeah, survivalists." He smiled, aware that she understood more than she let on. "They bring a great deal t' the group, with knowledge an' abilities. Plus, they're all single an' disconnected from th' outside world."

"That division is very important to you," she observed. "That everyone stay…aloof…from the rest of humanity."

"In a roundabout way, I guess you could say that. Don' get me wrong. We still need the rest o' the world so we can gather knowledge an' resources. But we're not really a part of it." He glanced down at her lips, noticing for the first time that she still wore no makeup. *Huh.*

"Take Kathy for instance," he continued. "We needed someone t' take care of our medical needs. I remember vividly when she left t' go t' nursin' school. It was a big deal. She was gone for two years, an' that's about the time we got the computers, an' everyone got on Facebook."

Bailey leaned closer, eager to hear more. "I wondered why you guys were putting up profiles. It doesn't seem odd to you?"

"I guess it does." He grinned at the memory. "I was already fourteen at the time, but my understanding o' life outside o' The Ranch had been severely limited. It was my first chance t' poke around an' learn about things beyond our four walls—stuff that hadn't been picked over an' watered down or censored.

"Anyways, we built the cyber network solely for the purpose o' keepin' her connected to us. After she came back, the *menfolk* discussed deleting everything since it had served its purpose. But they decided it was a good thing, an' it stuck, allowing us to communicate with each other when anyone leaves the group. Well, not leaves. No one really leaves…more like when they have to be away for a while." Frowning, he noticed that her expression had changed. "What?"

"*Menfolk*," she repeated, her brow crinkled. "The boys said that, and I thought it meant all of you, men-ly speaking, but hearing you say it, it sounds like something else."

"Yeah." He cracked a crooked smile. "It means th' elders. The seven men in charge o' the community."

Bailey counted on her fingers, quickly deducing who they were. "So that's your government. Not like a dictatorship."

"No." He exposed even more of his teeth for her. "I guess you could say *menfolk* is another way o' saying *council*, or somethin' like that."

Bailey grinned more broadly as well, a swarm of butterflies suddenly going nuts in her gut. "Ok, I get it. You can go on."

"Well, the *menfolk* basically run things. An' they make the choices that'll benefit the group as a whole." Drawing a deep breath, he exhaled loudly through a dropped jaw. "That's why it was decided that you would never hold a place among us. Because they as a group came to that choice."

Bailey looked stricken, butterflies squashed. "You mean my uncle had a say in that?"

"He had a vote, yes." The man across from her nodded. "An' I wasn't there when it was taken, so I don't know for sure which way he went, but one way or the other, the vote did not fall in your favor. An' that's how it goes. As soon as four of them agree on something, that's the way it is no matter how the other three feel about it."

Nodding, the girl continued to frown. "They were really going to kill me."

"Probably," his voice grew softer. "That's part o' their job, remember? They weren't just some random guys, little bit. They're mercenaries. Capable o' taking care o' whatever needs t' be done an' t' help defend the group if we ever need it."

"Wow," she gasped, her eyes on the table between them. "Then I've put everyone in a terrible place."

"It's not your fault. If your parent's hadn't gotten hit by that truck, you would've been at college…" *Shit.* He stopped speaking abruptly, causing the sentence to sound even more awkward.

"I would have been at college?" She lifted her gaze to his, noting the terrified expression that he seemed to be fighting to remove from his features. "Did you guys have something to do with my parents' accident?" She sat up straighter in her chair, her brow drawn into deep furrows.

"No," he denied flatly, his fingers making it to the edge of the table, tapping it nervously, aware that they had been discussing mercenaries two minutes before. "I really don' wanna talk about that, Bailey."

"You don't want to, but you are," she demanded, leaning towards him and stabbing the flat surface between them with a long digit. "I knew something wasn't right. I felt it in my gut! The car, the apartment, all the shit that was here waiting for them! You guys were after my brothers!"

Caleb smacked his lips noisily, his tongue flicking around his lips. "I told you before. You an' I are pawns. We do what th' *menfolk* designate." He held up a stiff index finger to cut off her torrent. "There's no use denyin' it. You've seen enough. You know what I'm talkin' about."

"Then tell me the truth," she begged, slumping back in the seat.

"Ok, the truth." He blew a puff of air into a cupped palm, rubbing the fingers together as if he were cold. "I…stalked your family. I was actually in town when the accident happened. The cops showin' up at your door that night scared the livin' shit outta me."

Her eyes grew wide, her voice evaporated, and all she could do was stare.

"They had noticed a couple of years ago that we were acutely short on boys. An' after Brenda got sick an' passed on, it was suggested that your uncle needed a new wife—younger wife, who might be able t' provide him with a few sons. That's when he spouted off an' suggested he could just borrow his nephews." He could see the terror in her eyes. "He didn't mean it, Bailey. It was a joke!"

"A joke," she breathed, the extent of her horror evident.

"Yeah, but once the idea was in the air, it jus' kinda hung there. An' grew. I had only been in town a couple o' weeks, gatherin' info about th' boys an' your parents…an' you." He shrugged. "To feel things out an' see what, if anything, could be done." He hung his head as he finished, aware that he might have been safer trying to explain Lawson than the can of worms he had opened.

"You people disgust me!" she spat vehemently.

"Yup, pretty much," he agreed wholeheartedly. "Brings a whole new meaning t' the words *the ends justifies th' means,* now don' it." He stared at her, watching her skin slowly shift, picking up a bright pink flush. "I really am sorry about your parents an' for everything that's happened."

"I bet you are." She had no control. "And I'm supposed to trust you…how? You are the scum of the earth! You are—"

"They have your brothers, Bailey," he stated calmly, nodding his head as if to agree with her assessment. Waiting half a minute, he gave her time to process his words. "I told you. We're the pawns. I do what they say, an' you do what they say. There is no good scenario here. You go t' school next week an' finish your senior year. Tha's the smart thing t' do."

"And if I don't choose to do the smart thing?"

"Then we can go get on my bike, an' I'll take you back, an' you can pray on th' way down they don't have a hole dug for your body when we get there."

The girl stared at her roommate for what seemed an eternity. He didn't speak, only returning her unwavering glare. Finally, she stood from her chair and made her way to her room, closing the door quietly and locking it. Shuffling over into the corner, she slid slowly down the wall, too awestruck to cry, too bewildered to think.

She knew the door wouldn't keep him out—not if he wanted in. *What does it matter?* she asked herself time and again, her mind turning in circles. She trembled in the darkness, waiting to fall asleep, waiting to awaken so the nightmare would end, waiting for the dawn so the next day could begin.

FIVE

Bad News, Baby

BAILEY AWOKE the following morning still pressed against the wood and sheetrock. Standing, she stretched, removing the stiffness from her limbs. Exiting her small sanctuary, she moved through the house, searching quietly for the man who shared her space. Unable to locate him, she stepped out onto the balcony, where she determined that his ride no longer sat parked in one of the spaces below.

Closing the door, she locked it, only briefly considering where he might be. *They have your brothers, Bailey.* She figured it didn't matter where he had gone; he would return. *We're the pawns, Bailey.* Going to her brothers' room, she turned on the computer, pulling up her Facebook page and new friends list.

One by one, she looked through the profiles, gathering every piece of information she could about the group. Eventually growing tired of the search, she shut down the machine, making her way to her room. Changing into her shorts and tee, she left the apartment, finding her way to the gym she had seen on her run the previous day.

Inside, she smirked at the equipment in disdain, ready to begin training in earnest. An hour later, she left, utterly exhausted. Back inside their refuge, she showered and dressed to go to the school, eager to double-check her registration and ensure that her senior year would go off without a hitch. Using her new bus pass for the round trip, she smiled to herself at her resourcefulness and ability to handle things. *I'm only a pawn if I allow myself to be.*

Shortly before five, the girl changed into her new uniform and walked over to her job, determined to make it through the shift. She wanted to pick up every hour she could so that her bank account would grow. Someday, she would need funds, and she allowed herself to dream about ways she might break her siblings out of the prison in which they were being held.

For ten days, she did not see Caleb. She knew that he came home each night and prepared himself a meal, but he did not go over to her work or disturb her in her room. In the mornings, he left quietly so he did not awaken her. As soon as the door closed, the girl dressed, headed for the gym and the training that would make her strong.

When school started, she had to find a way to include the exercise in her routine. Thankfully, she had two off periods in the afternoon, as she had completed all but a few of the courses required for graduation. Catching an earlier bus, she would be home in time to hit the gym, shower, and still make work by five if she were diligent in her timing. She felt driven to do this, and she used the image of the muscled blonde who had dented her forehead to drive her on, pure hate fueling her desire to prove the man who shared her space wrong.

Caleb took great care to avoid even a glimpse of silky auburn curls. His chest ached from the pain he had seen in her pure green eyes. Throwing himself into his employment, he went in early, stayed late, and almost forgot to register for his fall class. Picking up his book over at the junior college, he grimaced at the amount of work that lay ahead of him to finish the course by Christmas.

He had managed to keep things in line until the tenth day, when his phone rang on his ride home from work. Stopped at a red light, he glanced at the screen, able to see the name John Cross blinking back at him. Easing the bike onto the adjacent parking lot, he took the call. "Yeah."

"Hey, Caleb," a crisp female voice greeted from the other end.

"'Manda?"

"Yeah, it's me." She giggled, then drew a lengthy breath. "I got some bad news, baby."

His lungs clamped shut, and his heart stopped dead in his chest, fear gripping him like a vice. "What's wrong? What's happened?" he demanded loudly, holding his other ear closed to hear her over the traffic to his left.

"I'm pregnant," she announced from afar, "an' yur mamma's wantin' t' plan our weddin'."

"You're what?!?" he demanded loudly, then rushed on, "You know damn good an' well I ain' never touched you!" he hollered over the diesel next to him.

"Oh, I'm so glad you're happy, baby!" she cooed. "I can hear you're in a bad spot, so I'll call you later, hun. Love you!"

"'MANDA!" he screamed, then pulling the phone away from his ear, he could see she had ended the call. Shoving the device into his pocket, he eased back out into the rush-hour traffic that lasted from five to seven each day. Weaving more than he normally dared, he hurried home as quickly as he could get there, fuming every inch of the way.

Mounting the stairs, he reached his father's voicemail. "You call me back!" he demanded loudly.

Inside, he pulled off his clothes and jumped into a fast shower, listening for a ringtone the entire time. When the call didn't come, he pulled on clean clothes. Grabbing his book, he hit the door, eager to get across the street and order his dinner. *And talk to Bailey.* The idea was out before he recalled he hadn't spoken to her in over a week. The thought of how long it had been put a knot in the pit of his gut.

Arriving at the restaurant, he could see the frown on her face before he got to the register. Waiting in line, he hugged the huge volume to his chest, blowing noisily through pursed lips, time and again. Finally, at the front of the pack, he lay his newest nemesis on the counter and attempted a smile. "Hey."

Her posture stiff, she inquired, "What will you have?"

Giving her his order, he produced his debit card and waited. Receiving it back, he half-smiled again. "Could you come an' see me on your break?"

"I already had my break," she replied curtly, fighting the urge to cry.

Nodding, he picked up the text and cup, making his way over to fill his drink and find a seat. Removing his phone from his pocket, he laid it on the table before him, glaring at it. *Ring.* The device lay dark, silently taunting him, until he picked it up and opened his news feed.

The first post knocked the wind from his chest. Amanda had tagged him in a life event: *Amanda Knight and Caleb Cross are having a baby.* At that moment, a tray containing his dinner landed on his table, and he looked up anxiously, half expecting to see Bailey standing over him.

Blinking up at the young man, he mumbled, "Thank you." Then, twisting in his seat, he craned to see the girl still at the register, taking orders, her expression unchanged. *Fuck.* Making it to his feet, he only took a single step before he realized he couldn't interfere. He had to let her do her job, and he would talk to her after she had finished. And after he had had time to plan what he would say.

Returning to the vinyl cushion, he ran his fingers through his nearly dry spikes. *Damn.* Turning to the meal, he unwrapped the burger and scarfed it, then began picking at the fries. When his phone lit up and began to sing, he snatched it up, pushing open the door and accepting the call simultaneously. "What'n the hell's goin' on?"

"Hi, son," his father replied calmly.

"Is she really pregnant?" he demanded in a loud voice, moving away from the crowded tables and further down the walk.

"Yeah, she is. Kathy confirmed it! Congratulations!" his old man boasted.

"No! No, Dad, I have never…touched…that girl!" His heart beat wildly inside his chest. "So whatever little game you guys are up to, you can forget it!"

"We're plannin' t' have the weddin' at Thanksgiving." His father ignored the comment. "An' we're gonna put Don over there t' babysit the Dewitt girl," he continued matter-of-factly.

"Don? Are you kidding me?" Caleb became more agitated by the minute. "You're not doin' either o' those things. I'm here, an' I'm takin' care o' Bailey. An' I'm not marryin' 'Manda!" His mind raced. "What I will do is meet you at a doctor's office for a paternity test."

"Aww, son," the older man's voice dropped. "You know it really don' have t' be this way."

"Yeah, it does. Why can't you jus' leave us alone?"

"Is our secret safe?" his tone fell even more.

"Your secrets are safe, Dad." He sighed heavily. "She don' know much, an' what she does know, she ain' gonna share. She knows you hold two aces in th' hole."

His father began to laugh at the analogy. "Ai'ight, son, this's what I'll do. These girls are all about makin' their plans, but I'll have 'em hold off for a summer weddin'. Next summer. You jus' make sure you keep yur business in your pants, an' don' go gettin' anybody else knocked up. An' we'll see you at Christmas."

"I don't know if we can make it for Christmas," he stalled. "Let them plan the wedding for next June, an' I'll play along, ok?"

"There ya go, son."

Caleb could almost see the grin on his face.

"Tha's a good boy."

Ending the call, the tall blond pocketed the device and made his way back to the shop. Opening his book, he stared at the pages while he waited for the other shoe to drop.

SIX

Getting By

BAILEY EXITED the door and made for the light, only pausing for an instant when Caleb called from behind, "That baby's not mine."

"I don't care," she replied, moving towards her goal and placing one foot in front of the other. *I can't think about your problems.* Punching the button, she refused to look at him and stood facing the street.

"Yeah, well, I could really use a friend right now. A real one."

Hearing her own words tumble out of his mouth, she turned only enough to see that he stared straight ahead. The walk symbol lit up, and they both moved, taking wide strides and traversing the distance to their small apartment.

"Why should I be your friend?" she quipped when they reached the stairs.

"You shouldn't," he replied. "I have done nothin' t' deserve it." He reached to open the door for her, then closed it behind them and secured the lock before following her down the hallway.

"And why would she say the baby is yours if it isn't?" the girl continued to rant in a passive-aggressive fashion, turning her back on him as soon as she had spoken.

"I don't know." He stood behind her, staring at her long crimson highlights. "But I have a feelin' it's got somethin' t' do with you," his voice dropped to a loud whisper.

"With me," she spat the words. "What in the hell could it possibly have to do with me?" She swung around to face him, her locks floating for an instant, daring him to touch them.

He shrugged. "All I know is, right now, she an' my mother are plottin' my wedding, an' my father wants t' trade me for Don t' look after you."

"Don? Finch? Why would he want to look after me?" her tone remained dagger sharp.

"He wouldn't." Caleb's gaze dropped to her perfect pink lips. "An' I wouldn't trust him to." He stared at her, his chest heaving in deep, labored breaths.

Bailey scowled at him, feeling her resolve weakening. She had known many people in her lifetime, called more than she could count *friend*. No one had ever taken the time to know the girl hidden inside her perfect shell the way Caleb had. "So when are you getting married." She pushed the hair out of her face and turned back around. Her eyes burned, and although she needed to know, she didn't really want to talk about the subject.

"After your graduation, when we return t' The Ranch. That should give me plenty o' time t' prove she's lyin' an' get out of it."

"You sound pretty confident that you will. Are you sure that it isn't yours?" her tone continued to drop, her anger giving way to pain. *He's been with her...*

Caleb tightened his jaw, knowing it would be no use trying to explain. "I am," he replied softly and left it at that.

With a deep sigh, Bailey looked over her shoulder to give him a sidelong stare. "I want to get my brothers away from them. That's what matters most."

"Yeah." He tossed his arms across his chest. "I can see why. An'

I'll help you if I can. I don't expect you t' trust me, little bit. But I hope I can rebuild your faith in me." Unfolding his limbs, he turned his palms to the ceiling. "You've been a true friend t' me, Bailey. Better than I deserve. I swear to you I will make this right."

She could feel herself grow tense, being forced to admit she couldn't reach her goal alone. She needed him, liar or not. *Damn.* "I would like for you to train me. I want to know it all. The fighting, the guns, everything." She clenched her teeth, her rage tinting her skin.

"We got about nine months." He grinned slightly, having seen the chink in her armor. "I'm sure I can teach you quite a bit by then."

She grimaced at his smile, balling her fists to avoid striking him. She wanted to berate him, to punish him for the pain her family had endured. "Goodnight, Caleb." She refused to share her thoughts. Entering her chamber, she closed her door firmly behind her.

"Goodnight, Bailey." He stared at the portal, a heavy sigh escaping him before he turned away, shutting his own.

The following morning, both were out of bed and in the kitchen early, each wearing their workout clothes. "When do they open the gym?" she demanded curtly.

"At five." He flicked his watch to take a peek. "We're good."

Making their way across the compound, they spent almost an hour going through what she had already learned and refreshing her assignment of moves to practice. He could feel her tension, aware that her mood had not improved. Walking back to the house, he quietly observed, "You've already been working out, haven't you?"

"Yes. I told you. I want my brothers back."

"An' you didn't think about…jus' callin' the police an' askin' for help?"

Arriving at their home, she decided to make breakfast before she bothered with a shower. Pulling out a skillet and putting eggs and bacon on the counter, she sighed. "I don't think they would be that helpful. You have to know that a bunch of people living in the desert, preparing for the end of the world sounds crazy. Saying that they murdered your parents to steal your little brothers, even more so."

"We didn't hurt your parents," he defended, holding up a hand. "Jus' throwin' that out there. They died in an accident, little bit."

"You say that"—she exhaled loudly—"but you know it doesn't end there. You can't tell me it wouldn't have happened the next year. I'm sure that's what all the *you would've been in college* business is about."

He shook his head. "I can't say either way. We had only started pokin' around when it happened." Reaching for plates, he sat at the table and made the toast.

"So," she returned to the subject when they were seated, "no, I don't plan on enlisting the help of the police. Mainly because as soon as I open my mouth and they start asking questions, the boys get hurt. I can't risk that."

"Is that why you didn' take off?" He waited, but she didn't respond, so he elaborated. "After our talk two weeks ago, I figured you'd run."

"There wasn't any point, and again, they would be hurt if I did. But at the same time, I wondered the same thing about you. Why you didn't go home since you obviously love it there. I can take care of myself. You could leave me here alone. Or are you really here to keep tabs on me?"

"I don't love it there," his tone held disgust. "It's my home. The only real life I've ever known. That bein' said, I can also admit it's a little messed up. An' no, I'm not keepin' tabs." He stared at her, his features grim as he grew quiet. "I really am lookin' out for you."

Bailey lifted her gaze, glaring with wide green eyes. "So…what? You've just been getting by? Not really a part of them?"

He looked away, breaking her hold on him. "Don't you see how hard this is for me?" his voice cracked, and he cleared his throat. "I don' know how long it's been this way. I only know that there's things I would change if I could. I'm tired o' bein' the pawn. I tol' you. I will make this right. I'll help you train, an' I'll help you try t' get 'em back. It won' be easy, but we'll do whatever we can do."

Reaching for the remote, he switched on the news, allowing it to play quietly in the background while he finished his meal, officially ending their uncomfortable conversation.

SEVEN

Eye on the Prize

THE FOLLOWING morning during her bus ride to school, Bailey thought about the goals she had previously held when her parents were alive. *None of it is going to happen.* She sniffed slightly while frowning at the cars passing by her window. She had accepted that her old life was gone forever, but it still hurt. *Getting Jase and Jess back —that's what I have to do.*

She exited the transport and muddled through her day, her mind distracted by the idea and returning to it often. By the time she sat back in her seat headed for home, she felt confident that freeing her siblings held top rank on her list of priorities, with getting her diploma only a close second.

Making her way into the apartment to change, she envisioned completing the year and immediately after graduation doing precisely that. *I'm not sure how yet, but I'll figure it out.* Caleb had said he would help her, and that gave her at least some hope that it could be done.

Stepping into the gym, she mentally planned her workout. Setting the treadmill for a warm-up run, her thoughts turned to the muscular man who shared her space. *You still can't trust him,* she informed herself tersely. *Not yet, if ever.* He had claimed the night before that he was going to make everything right, but she found that hard to believe, especially since his dishonesty continued to be a major concern.

At the same time, she knew she would have to put up a front, as her mother called it, and at least behave civilly towards him. *Otherwise, he won't help you.* She sighed, climbing off the machine and setting up a weight bar for a few sets of lifting. Her thoughts continued to churn while she drove herself to exhaustion and decided she had had enough for the day—both of exercise and of men.

Back at the house a short time later, she showered and donned her uniform, making her way to the shop and taking a seat in the lobby until time to clock in. Staring up at the large screen, her foul mood continued as she read the captions on the silent set, her nose wrinkled at the mundane program. *I can't believe they installed a television while I was gone. It's pathetic. People can't even eat without being entertained.*

Rising, she made her way to the back. "Hey, Mark," she addressed her boss tentatively. "Would you mind if I changed the program out front?"

"Naw. The remotes under the counter. But remember, if a customer requests a different station, you'll have to keep them happy," he informed her with a grin.

Returning the small smile, she replied crisply, "I always do, right? So yes, I will, and thanks." Locating the tuner, she flipped through until she located a national news program. Retaking her seat, she stared up at the flickering screen while the anchor ranted about stocks and money matters.

Glancing around at the lobby, none of the few patrons that were dining at the early hour even seemed to notice the switch. When the time came to take her place at the register, she returned the remote, prepared to make the adjustment should the need arise as the evening wore on.

No one ever asked, so the girl picked up the habit of making the change every night when she came in. It appeared that the customers paid little attention to what was on the set or simply watched it anyways. On a rare occasion, one would, but for the most part, the girl kept it there, able to view what was going on in the world between running the register and on her break.

In this way, her days soon ran together, as each one felt incredibly like the last. Driven by what lay ahead, Bailey wouldn't have described her life as happy—far from it. She merely grew comfortable with her arrangement and pushed herself each day, doing what was necessary to reach the next step. By the end of September, she had become fully absorbed in her goals and routine, content to tackle each day as it came at her, while keeping her eye on the prize.

Caleb, on the other hand, fought constantly with his inner demons and had been since he met her. Living with her as his only companion did nothing to relieve the stress it had caused. He worked with her each morning, teaching her and watching her grow and change in her slow transformation. He saw her in the evenings, and although everything appeared fine between them, he could sense her tolerance and missed her friendship.

Throwing himself headlong into his studies, he pushed to finish the course by Thanksgiving, knowing they would have more time afterwards to further her understanding of weapons and their uses. Keeping himself busy gave him something to do as well and helped to alleviate some of the emptiness he felt since she had backed away.

Before they had fled The Ranch, he had thought they might have had a future and built a life together. But since their return to Midland, since his role in things had been revealed, he had grown certain he would never be more to her than he had been. *She will never get past the part I have played—or I won't.* He would help her get her family back and see to it she would have a chance to have a good life. *To find her Mr. Right.*

At the beginning of October, Caleb decided it was time to take

Bailey to the next step, in her training at least. Choosing a bookstore, he pulled into the parking lot after work and made his way inside. Grinning to himself while recalling her progress, he located a selection of texts filled with detailed pictures and explanations of pistols and rifles. Purchasing the lot, he dropped them into a saddlebag and weaved his way home through the typical traffic. Taking in the gym, he prepared his meal after his shower, turning on the television as usual.

After cleaning up his mess, he stretched out in the recliner end of the sofa, flipping through the glossy pages of one of the new books he intended to present to her when she arrived home. *You should be studying,* he reprimanded himself, quickly dismissing the idea. *I've been workin' my ass off for weeks. One night o' rest ain't gonna kill me.*

The news on in the background, his eyes shot up to stare at the screen. *Did they say earthquake?* He soon discovered the disaster had taken place on the west coast only a few hours before, and relief groups were already taking care of the situation. Setting the book aside, he used the remote, increasing the volume to pick up the details and remained glued to the screen until Bailey bolted through the door at the end of her shift.

"Did you hear?" She sounded breathless, tossing her purse on the ottoman and turning to lock the door behind her.

"About that?" He wafted the controller towards the screen. "Yeah, I heard."

Perching on the opposite end of the sectional, the girl leaned on her arm, chewing lightly on her finger. "I've been watching it down at the shop all night. It happened about five thirty, our time."

"Yeah." He glanced over at her agitated state. "Relax, little bit. It's only an earthquake. They get 'em all the time, an' they know what t' do. See? They already have the emergency response in full swing."

"I know," she breathed. "But they were talking about a tsunami hitting some place as a result and all the damage and loss of life that will result. Maybe California really is going to fall off into the ocean," she teased, recalling the volcano that had opened up south of the state only a few months prior.

"I doubt it." He laughed at her. "It ain't that serious. Trust me. Here. I got you somethin'." He leaned over and pushed the stack towards her across the cushion. "Maybe it'll take your mind off o' global disaster."

Tearing her eyes away from the screen, she slid down and retrieved the pile. "What's all this?"

"Books," he replied crisply, as if she couldn't tell, "about weapons. You said you wanted t' learn it all. Or have you changed your mind about that?"

"Oh, no." She shook her head, opening one of the large flat texts. "I do want to learn."

"Good. 'Cause I think you're ready for th' next step."

"Am I?" She glanced at him, noting his serious expression. "Then I guess so. I'll have to do it here though." She grimaced at the size of it. "I can't take it to school, or someone might turn me in as a nutcase." She giggled at the idea of gleaning such a label.

"Yeah," he shared in her amusement. "If they only knew."

Cutting her eyes over at him, she held the smile, her mind turning what he might have meant. Perusing the rest, she nodded. "Well, thank you. They appear very informative. I really like the pictures, too." She ran her fingers over a shiny revolver. "I'll do my best to get through them quickly. Without all the college prep stuff, school has turned into a breeze."

"Whadda you mean?" he gasped slightly, sitting up straighter. "What happened to all your college prep courses? You're still goin', aren't you?"

Bailey gaped at him with her jaw hanging. *Crap.* "Oh, I don't know." Her face crinkled. "I've been thinking about that. After I get the boys away from Uncle Pete, I'll have to keep working and maybe get a better job—or two jobs, even—to support us. But it's ok. I can still go to college without those courses even if I have to wait until the twins are grown to do it." She forced a nervous smile, not comfortable discussing her plans for the future with him. "It'll work out."

Tossing the books aside, she returned her eyes to the screen, ready to steer the conversation in a more suitable direction. "That's kind of ironic." She indicated the newscast with an extended digit. "We have a post going about natural disasters. I wonder if the girls have seen this yet."

"A post goin'?" he feigned ignorance. "With who?"

"The girls from The Ranch, silly!" She cut herself off before she referred to them as *the nice list*.

"Oh, yeah, them," he exaggerated the words, teasing her about her growing comfort with the community members. "Maybe you should point it out to 'em in case they missed it." He grinned while she got to her feet to do precisely that.

Exiting the boys' room a few minutes later, she returned to gather her books, noting he still seemed engrossed in the drama playing out before them. "No one had mentioned it, so I made a new post and tagged everyone."

"Nice." He stood, cutting off the announcer abruptly. "Well, I gotta get t' bed. I gotta be in at six tomorrow for an early job, so you're on your own in th' mornin'."

"Aww, another one?" she teased, entering her room. She hated to admit it, but she was becoming comfortable with him again, despite her efforts to keep him at bay. Placing the books on her desk, she caressed the edge of one. *He can be so thoughtful.*

Slipping off her shoes, she noticed a large black spot on the wall above the head of her bed and announced loudly, "Damn, I have a spider." Lifting one of the sneakers, she prepared to deal with the beast. "Wow, it's funny looking. All bumpy...err fuzzy..." Her voice trailed away.

"Bumpy?" Caleb called from the room across the hall, realizing what it meant at the same instant he heard the scream. Closing the distance between them in a dash, he caught the girl in mid spasm. Whacking at the arachnid had caused it to fall, and a spray of tiny spider replicas had scattered across her pillow and bedding.

Caleb guided her out of the way while Bailey waved her hands about wildly. Her auburn hair flew around her head as she flailed and cried out, "Oh, God, get them off! Get them off!"

"I don' think they're on you." He laughed, trotting into the kitchen to retrieve the insecticide from under the sink. Back in her room, he doused the covers as best he could while she inspected herself in the bathroom mirror, checking for bugs.

"I can feel them, Caleb!" she whined loudly, oblivious to the neighbors she more than likely had disturbed.

"Prolly not," he corrected. "You're worked up, tha's all." He moved in beside her, taking a look for himself. Standing still, she allowed him to part some of the long strands and view her scalp. "Why did you hit it?" he demanded sternly, holding his snickers in check.

"Because," she snapped, "I didn't know it was covered in babies!"

"Well, now you know. Bumpy an' fuzzy mean *don't touch*," he reprimanded while trying not to laugh. Pushing her head back, he peered down into her face. His thumb grazed her flushed cheek, her green eyes wide with adrenaline. "Get in th' shower, little bit," he breathed softly. "Wash your hair. I don' think there's any in there, but it'll put your mind at ease."

In silent agreement, the girl reached over and turned on the tap, returning to her room to gather her sleeping attire and glare at the bed. "I guess it's the sofa for me tonight," she announced loudly, closing the bathroom door behind her.

Exiting with a puff of steam a few minutes later, Bailey dried her dripping hair with a towel. Prepared to slumber on the sectional, she discovered Caleb seated upon it. "I thought you were going to bed!"

"Me too, but some shrieking woman has got me all excited." He grinned at her deviously. Having quieted his spasms of laughter while she bathed, his breathing had returned to normal, and he hoped he passed for concerned. "You can share with me." He stood, indicating the room at the end of the hall. "It's a king, an' there's no reason I can't stay on my half an' you on yours, at least for one night." He nodded, guiding her to the entrance of his chamber. "You can wash your sheets an' stuff tomorrow."

Bailey frowned, eyeing the wide mattress reluctantly. "Are you sure?" she sighed. "I don't want to put you out."

"Naw, it's fine." He continued to grin. "That's your half, an' this's mine." He used his hands to divide the accommodations. Cutting off the light, he slid into his section, calling firmly, "Goodnight, Bailey."

Dropping the towel over the foot of the bed, the girl timidly followed suit, listening to the man breathe in the darkness. Before long, she could tell he had fallen asleep, so she rolled over and observed him in the dim light.

Making out his face in the soft glow, she chuckled quietly to herself at the commanding way he had handled the incident. *Pretty funny, actually. That's the second time he's saved me.* She continued to smile, drifting off to sleep with visions of her knight in shining armor running through her head.

EIGHT

When it Rains

CALEB AWOKE THE NEXT MORNING, dimly aware of the female body pressed against his. Panic washed over him, his pulse pounding in his ears, and he struggled to keep his movements slow and calm so as not to wake her. His touch gentle, he fumbled beneath the covers to discover she remained fully dressed, with her back to him. Heaving a sigh of relief, he sank back onto his pillow and stared at the ceiling above them, waiting for his nerves to calm.

Sliding an arm over her waist and across her belly, he spooned up behind her, nuzzling his face into her soft auburn curls. *She must have scooched over next to me in the night.* His breathing returning to normal, he closed his eyes. *She didn't mean anything by it.* His fingers tracing her lower ribs through her cotton shirt, his mind wandered, leaping to what lay hidden beneath it. *I could get used to this.*

His eyes shot open at the thought, and he worked his way off the bed. Quickly gathering clean apparel, he dodged into the bathroom. *Shit.* Dropping the articles onto the sink, he cranked on the shower full blast and stripped down to climb beneath the frigid spray. *That was stupid,* he berated himself as the cold water poured over his scalp and ran down his smooth back.

Leaning his head against the wall, he pressed the palm of his left hand flat against it. Spitting a few times, his mind retraced the night before and how he had allowed himself to make the offer. *Damn, you almost blew it, mister.* Closing his eyes, he struggled to breathe, hoping she still slept and would remain unaware of his desire to cop a feel.

Outside the small chamber, Bailey lay in the darkness, listening to the cascade. Her mind briefly succumbed to the idea that he was naked, and she envisioned the bare chest she had seen a few times, along with more private areas. *He didn't stay on his side*, and she had awoken in his embrace.

A few seconds later, her thoughts shifted to Ked and his grasping manner, darkening her mood. *Yup, he's a guy after all.* Sliding out of the covers, she darted into her room.

Not bothering with a shower, she hurriedly slipped into her workout clothing. Comparing the two males, she found Caleb's behavior odd, in that he seemed to hold the same desires as her former would-be boyfriend. However, he also appeared to be working very hard at keeping them under wraps rather than pushing her to join him in the naughty behavior. *Or is he biding his time until he's ready to spring it on me?* The thought made her uneasy, whichever way she took it.

Desiring to be gone when her roommate left for work, she exited the apartment and climbed onto a treadmill inside the gym. After her run, she did stretches and practiced moves for the rest of the hour, waiting there until after six before she felt certain he would no longer be at home to greet her. Making her way across the compound, she breathed deeply, calming herself after the vigorous workout.

Inside the kitchen a few minutes later, she removed eggs and scrambled them for breakfast. Being her Friday off at work, she considered skipping school and taking the whole day as a gift to herself. *Time to relax and do some things for me.* The idea tempted her strongly after the stress she had been under as of late.

Sauntering down the hall, she stood next to her crumpled bed, staring down at the small black specks that had not escaped the poison. Deciding having a day for her own would be justified, she changed into ordinary jeans and a T-shirt after her shower. Stripping down the bed, she shoved the items into a basket and gathered the soap and quarters to take care of the necessities first.

Choosing one of the new books to read while she waited, she made her way to the laundry and set up the machine. Sitting on the folding table, she leaned her back against the wall while she flipped the pages slowly, taking in the details of the small caliber weapons. *Mom and Dad didn't believe in guns,* she recalled as she traced the outline of one in particular.

Reading the description, she discovered that it was a powerful model with a hard kick, and she wondered briefly what it would be like to fire such a thing. Her curiosity wetted, she stood and moved over to the window. Glaring out at the buildings that obstructed her view, she knew the road lay on the other side. *Across the street is that strip mall with my work, some other things...and an Academy Sports department store.*

"Academy," she spoke aloud, a flicker of an idea forming in the back of her mind. "This is my day, and I can do what I want with it."

Back in Illinois, Bailey had enjoyed a few such days when Pamela Dewitt had had a clear schedule or a canceled court date and had chosen to spend it with her daughter. She would pick her up from school a few hours early, and the pair would go shopping, selecting the styles that had kept her slender frame ahead of the pack in the fashion department.

That, or they would have made a trip to a salon, where a good manicure and pedicure could be found. Bailey had cherished those outings, since her mother had rarely spent time with her alone. In fact, the girl could count maybe a dozen of the instances total, and that made them all the more special.

Her blankets buzzing loudly, the dryer announced the day's chore was half complete, and she hauled the load upstairs to remake her bed. Once it had been accomplished, she checked herself in the mirror and located her purse to retrieve her wallet, ready to see a few of the weapons firsthand.

Flipping through the book to make a short list of the most interesting ones, she shoved it into her pocket and stomped down the stairs. Crossing at the light, she smiled as she passed in front of her store, the patio already dotted with patrons enjoying an early lunch. It may have been the first week of October and too cold for dining outdoors back home, but here, they would see ninety or better for the day's high, and therefore the area remained popular.

Her mind drifting back to their arrival last spring, she recalled that the weather had been warm then, as well. *I bet this place doesn't get any sort of winter at all,* she sighed. Arriving at her destination, she entered through the sliding glass doors and located the gun cases on the far-right hand side of the sales floor.

Pulling out her list, she peered through the glass, making her way along and reading the place cards until she had located one of them. "Excuse me," she called softly to the man on the other side of the counter. "I'd like to see this nine-millimeter pistol, please."

The back side of the sales area being raised, the man towered above her, causing his glower to appear even more menacing as it poured down upon her. "You gotta be twenty-one t' purchase a handgun," he informed her bluntly. "You got an ID?"

"Oh!" She took a step back in surprise. "I'm not here to buy it!" Her mind turning, she realized her blunder and that her chances were growing slim that she would reach her goal that day. "I'm doing a research project on them…for school," she began to fabricate a cover story, her mind swirling. "And I was curious how it felt to hold one."

The dark-haired man stared at her, unmoved by her explanation. Blinking at her for a long moment, he eventually cast his gaze up and down the counter. "Well," he commented half to himself, "it's a slow mornin'. An' you're not actually makin' a purchase." Pulling out a key, he opened the small gliding door and lifted the weapon. "Careful with it. It's a little heavy."

Gingerly taking it, Bailey's fingers trembled slightly. "Wow, it is," she agreed with a small smile. Thinking quickly, her brow furrowed. "How do you decide which one you should buy?"

"Well, that depends." He reached to retrieve the pistol and return it to its stand. "You definitely want one that fits your hand an' feels good when you hold it. But you also wanna choose one that'll suit your needs, not too big or too small."

"Too big or too small," she repeated, observing more of the inventory while she listened. "You mean the bullets, right?"

"Yeah, the bullets." He shrugged, noting the customer that had appeared behind her. "Can I help you, sir?" He dismissed the girl unceremoniously, and she moved away, her eyes roving over the selection of rifles and shotguns that lined the wall behind him.

Spending close to half an hour with the man, the clerk ignored her. Standing quietly, she observed as the transaction took place, feeding her curiosity over all of the requirements and paperwork that went into making a purchase. Once the sale had been completed, she decided it would be worth a Google search that afternoon so she could gather more information on that subject as well.

Returning home to prepare her lunch, Bailey carried her sandwich into the boys' room and perched at the desk. Biting into the meat and bread, she flicked on the computer and watched it come to life. Pulling up her profile, she read through the posts, looking over the latest comments from the nice list and typing a few of her own. Only a few had noticed the post about the earthquake, and it appeared it would take a few days for the discussion to develop.

Her routine checking-in completed and her lunch gone, she sat back in her chair and studied the screen. She hadn't dug through the community profiles in weeks, but she recalled having seen a few of them holding weapons in some of their posts. Sitting up straight, she began to work her way through their pics, curious now that she had an idea of what she was looking at.

After a few minutes of skimming, she located one. Opening the books, she identified the weapon and smiled to herself. *Wow, I am learning.* Continuing her search, she discovered that many of the community members could be found holding various models, one of which was Caleb. Obviously taken several years ago, the younger version of him stood over an enormous deer carcass.

Locating the rifle he held in his right hand, she discovered that his was called an SKS. *He sure looks pleased with himself.* She smiled along with the photo. *I bet the meat had gone a long way towards feeding the community, too.* Laying her fingers across the screen, she thought of the boys and how they had also been learning to be proficient at using them. *Little men.*

With a small sigh, she resumed her search, finding more pictures and soon realizing all of the girls and women also had their favorites. *Caleb wasn't kidding when he said everyone had been trained.* A moment later, her heart stopped cold for an instant before it began beating wildly inside her chest.

Before her, a shot of Amanda, posted by Kristen Tate, stared back at her. Clicking the smaller image, she enlarged it to get a better look. Spying the date, she realized it had been taken over a year ago, presumably while she and Caleb had still been dating. The idea of it bothered her, and she could feel the angry flush rising from her chest to wash over her neck and face. *What a bitch.*

Amanda had been posting for weeks how deeply in love she and Caleb were—how long they had known their wedding would come. The image of the girl with the two men made Bailey seethe with rage. *How can she make such a claim after behaving in such a manner?*

Flicking the mouse, she removed the photo, but it remained burned into her mind, and it occurred to her for the first time that Caleb might be telling the truth. The idea startled her. Even though she had not been so rude as to rub it in his face, she really had not believed anything he had said to her since their arrival back in Midland.

I guess she's not the only one who's been treating him unfairly, she admonished herself. She gathered her trash and shut down the machine. *Well, when it rains, it pours.* Deep down, she knew she had been cold-hearted towards the man who obviously cared about her, taking nothing he told her with any ounce of confidence. *I guess I've been a real bitch as well.*

The realization sent her pulse into overdrive for the second time that afternoon. Dropping the refuse into the bin, she stared at the kitchen for a moment, considering how she could make amends. *You know he cares and looks out for you.* However, she declined to label her roommate's behavior as anything stronger than friendship, even after what had passed between them overnight. *You'd be foolish to get caught up in it, whatever it means.*

But the way he held me this morning, she challenged her resolve. Her memories returned in a flood, and she could not quell the excitement they produced. *He wasn't touching anything he shouldn't have been, unlike Ked, who put his hands all over me...every chance he got.* She thought of the younger man angrily.

Deciding to make the chicken-fried steaks that he loved, she removed meat from the freezer to thaw while her mind raced. *His warm breath moving across my ear, his fingers tickling my belly.* It had been exciting whether she had wanted it to be or not. *Damn. That's exactly how you got into trouble last time.*

She wasn't sure which had awakened her, but he must have noticed, because he had jumped up and fled to the shower. *Maybe he's as scared as you are,* she admitted the reason for her flight to the gym.

Or maybe he doesn't want to be anything more than friends. The idea gave her chill bumps. Of course, to know for sure she would have to ask him, and that would be out of the question. *You should leave it alone and pretend it didn't happen. You have more important things to worry about.*

She made batter to coat the steaks, her mind seemingly trapped and unable to let the issue go. *One thing's for certain. He really is my friend.* She hadn't thought of him as such in months. While she coated and floured their meal, she turned and sifted through her memories of the time she had known Caleb Cross.

Her emotions rose and fell, as there had been good times between them—real and honest times, during which she had shared thoughts and ideas she never trusted to anyone. But in the end, there had been painful times as well. Putting the finishing touches on her surprise, she realized many of those were beyond his control. *We're the pawns, Bailey.* She sighed at his description of their situation.

But he's tired of being a pawn. Struggling to clear the idea away, she reminded herself again, *You need to stay away from him. You can't get caught up in him...or his life.*

Catching her breath, she gave the open door a startled glare. "Oh, hello!"

Stopped in mid-motion, Caleb noted her strained expression and slowly removed his key from the lock. "Hey," he replied quietly. "You off tonight?"

"Yes, as a matter of fact I am." She nodded confirmation. "I made dinner for you. The gravy will be ready in about five minutes."

"Ok. I'll wash up real quick an' be right back," he supplied, heading for the back of the house. *Dinner for me, huh?* He briefly considered if it might be poisoned.

Making it down the hall, he could feel his heart bouncing around in his chest. He had been plagued by guilt over his behavior the entire day, largely because she had run from the apartment while he bathed. Rolling up his sleeves, he removed the grey powder from his arms and hands. Smoothing a squirt of lotion on them, he returned to the table and stared down at the dishes she placed before him, too anxious to dig in.

"Listen, uh…before we eat, I wanted to apologize t' you," he stammered, "for my behavior this mornin'."

Staring at him wide-eyed, the girl sank into the seat across from him. "Why? Did you do something I don't know about?" She swallowed noticeably, the amount of time she had spent thinking about his actions putting her on edge.

"I don't know." He served his plate. "I promised I wasn't gonna touch you, an' I shouldn't have."

"Don't worry about it, Caleb," she offered quietly. "I mean, friends can snuggle, can't they?" She forced a nervous grin, taking a steak for herself.

"Yeah, they can," he faltered at her smile. "But I don' want you readin' too much into it." He surveyed the meal she had prepared.

"I'm not reading anything into it." She cut her eyes over at him cautiously, holding the expression in place.

"Well, you left before I was even outta the shower…" his voice trailed away. "I thought you mighta been pissed."

"No." She giggled in relief. "I wasn't pissed. I mean, it surprised me." She shrugged. "When I woke up, you were holding me, but that's as far as it went that I know of. Or did something else happen before that?" She grew tense. "Did I do something…to you? Is that why you left in such a hurry?"

"No, little bit. I had t' get my shower before work," he lied flatly, "an' that's all that happened. But I shouldna touched you. I don' want you t' think I'd ever take advantage o' you."

Bailey laughed out loud, pausing between bites. "It's ok, Caleb. We're friends, remember? I trust you. I mean that."

His breath escaped in a loud gasp, and he picked up his knife and fork, his appetite gripping him full force. "Well, tha's a relief." He chuckled. "Here I thought you'd be fuming at me all day." Taking a few bites, his heart rate returned to normal. "I'm glad we're friends again, Bailey-girl. I've really missed you. An' this is great stuff by the way!" He pointed at his plate with his fork, his grin spread from ear to ear.

She stared at him after his confession. *He missed me?* Holding her front in place, she nodded. "Yes, I've missed you, too." *Oh, shit! Maybe I had him pegged right after all... He really is a guy...just like Ked.*

NINE

Mother Nature

THE FOLLOWING MORNING, the couple made their way to the gym early for her training before Caleb left for work. Neither of them found much to say after their eventful previous day, which left an uneasy cloud hanging between them. Grabbing a quick shower while she cooked, he scarfed the breakfast and made his way to the door. "I'll see you tonight, little bit," he called to her cheerily as he exited, leaving her to clean up the mess.

After he was gone, Bailey tried not to think about their relationship; she had spent enough time worrying over it. However, since her discovery, she could see Amanda for who she really was, and that had changed things for her on so many levels. She felt deeply concerned about the man the other girl had used, and would still hurt, until they could get the whole situation sorted out.

Realizing she was about to waste another day worrying about things she could not change, she mentally put her foot down. *You will stop this instant.* Placing items in the dishwasher, she turned on a music station rather than the news, ready to focus on cleaning the house until it was time to go to work. Soon, the tunes had put her more at ease, and she felt a sense of pride at taking care of their household.

Making a trip to the laundry, she took his clothes as well as her own. A small smile painted her lips as she shoved his into the first machine. She had never done so before, forcing him to take care of his wardrobe as best he could between his long hours at work and the time he spent studying. *He said we were in this together,* she rationalized, recalling his comment when he gave her the money for her phone. For the first time since their arrival, she actually believed it.

A short time later, she carried their items back to the apartment, hanging up and placing them in drawers accordingly. That task complete, she set about the bathrooms, then the bedrooms, and even gave the kitchen a thorough scrubbing, as well. She left for work shortly before five, beside herself with joy at what she had accomplished.

When Caleb arrived home that evening, the fresh smell of pine-scented cleanser greeted him at the door, indicating her latest cleaning spree. He smiled his approval at her efforts while glancing around at how neat and well-kept everything seemed to be. Strolling down the hall, he entered his room, his pleased expression fading at discovering his laundry basket sat empty and his own room was spotless.

Surveying the closet, his features took on an actual frown, as it appeared that all of his things had been washed and put away. *Well, fuck. This ain't gonna work,* he chastised the girl's efforts. Keeping it to a short shower, he passed on the computer and gathered his schoolwork to take over to the shop.

Arriving at the counter a short time later, he stared calmly into her clear green eyes, noting she seemed in good spirits. Accepting his card from her, he nodded. "Come an' see me on your break?"

"Sure." Her lips curled, and she shooed him away to help the next in line with a giggle.

Watching her take the next order while he filled his cup with ice and soda, an uneasy feeling settled in the pit of his gut. He knew he would have to handle this gently if he didn't want to damage their mending relationship. Plopping his book on the table, he briefly considered not even mentioning it at all. *But I can't. I have to say something before it gets out of hand.*

When the time came for her to eat, Bailey gathered her dinner and carried it to the lobby, taking the seat opposite the tall blond. Careful not to disturb his papers, she unwrapped her dinner and began to nibble at the burger and fries.

"Thank you for doing my laundry," he stated quietly without taking his eyes off the page before him. "It'll save me some time." Lifting his gaze, he studied her. "But you don' have t' do that," he finished quietly.

"I know," she agreed between bites. "It was my way of thanking you—for the spider assistance. Besides, you said we were in this together, so I figured I could be doing more."

Caleb stared at her, his gut twisting into a knot. "Bailey, I don' wanna play house with you."

Her jaw dropped, she stared at him. "Play house?" Her breath hung in her chest. "What's that supposed to mean?"

"It means I can do my own laundry." He struggled to keep the edge out of his voice. "I like the way you keep everything clean, an' I get that you like things a bit more tidy than mos' people. But I gotta draw the line at takin' care o' my personal stuff. I'm not mad that you did, but you're not my maid." *Or my wife,* he mentally challenged. "An' I'd rather you left my stuff alone."

The girl gaped at him. "I see," she breathed. "Well, I'm glad we got that cleared up. May I eat my dinner, or is there anything else you wanted to say?"

Running his fingers through his hair, he sighed, knowing he had upset her. "No, that's it. I'm sorry if I hurt your feelings." He glanced at the television above her. "But after what happened yesterday, I jus' wanna keep the boundaries clear. You an' I are good friends, an' I don' wanna do anything that'll mess that up."

Taking a few more bites of her hamburger, she chewed slowly. Switching to French fries, she quietly agreed, "I guess you're right, and I didn't think about it that way. I have no intention of *playing house* with you. I wanted to step up and be a better teammate, that's all."

Emitting a small laugh, he continued to watch the broadcast above her head. "Ok, little bit. I'll buy that. An' I do appreciate it." He decided not to push the subject any further in the public place, but nothing she had said had cleared his conscience over the issue. Noticing the scroll at the bottom of the screen, he groaned, "Did you hear about the earthquake?"

"Yeah, goofy. We talked about it days ago."

"Not that." He indicated the television. "The one today."

Swallowing quickly, Bailey gulped her soda to wash down the bite. "Another one?"

"Yeah." Closing his papers inside his book, he slid to the right. "Come look."

Switching sides of the table, she leaned her head back, absently eating a few more fries while watching the words slide by. "Wow. Nine-point-three, so it's the second largest ever recorded. And I bet there will be another tsunami to follow."

"That's generally how it works," he agreed softly. "Mother nature at her finest. O' course, FEMA was already crawlin' all over the place, helpin' out victims. This'll only add t' th' chaos."

Bailey could see his jaw tighten. "You don't think they're really helping?"

"Oh no, they're helpin'," he agreed. "They're doin' what they can." His voice grew distant. "We got another huge hurricane comin' into Florida tomorrow night—which makes three big storms this season so far. I'm wonderin' what the government's gonna do about that. FEMA's stretched thin t' say the least." Glancing at her long auburn locks, he smiled. "Eat your dinner, little bit. This's nothin' new an' no sense worryin' over it."

"You say that a lot," she accused, her brow furrowing. "But I get the feeling you do."

"Do what?"

"Worry," she countered evenly. "So go on. Spit it out."

Stretching in an exaggerated manner, he gave her a half-grin. "Not right now. Maybe tonight, after you get off."

"Are you going home then?" She gathered her trash to get back to work.

"Naw. I'm gonna hang out here an' study. Walk you home an' all that." He winked at her with a grin.

"Ok, then I'll see you after a while." Leaving him to his book, the girl did her best to immerse herself in the flow of customers, only periodically stealing a glance at the screen. However, her mind would not let go of the issue he had presented her, and by the time her boss locked the door behind her, she couldn't wait any longer to ask.

"How many people work for FEMA?" she demanded as soon as they were walking down the path to the light.

"Come on." He laughed. "Have you been thinkin' about that all night?"

"Yes, as a matter of fact I have, so how many?"

Shaking his head, he stared at the signal, waiting for it to change. "About ten thousand," he replied softly. "But that's not th' problem."

"Ok, what is the problem?"

Glancing at the girl next to him, he reached over and clasped her fingers lightly in his. "Why do you wanna know?"

"Because"—she could feel the anger beginning to grow—"I'm as concerned about the future as you and your crazy friends are," she spat, yanking her digits free. Putting a stiff finger in his face at the bottom of the stairs, she hissed, "You know, just when I think I can trust you, you go all secretive on me, and then I feel like you're lying to me again!"

"I tol' you before, I never lied t' you." He indicated the steps with his left hand. "Le's take this inside at least." Once the door had closed behind him, he worked the lock, pausing before he faced her. "It's the fact that we have never had or needed such a group, but today we do. Have you ever wondered why?"

"No." She sighed, dropping her purse on the couch and kicking off her shoes, exhausted from her full day of chores and work.

"It's because we've had more natural disasters in th' last twenty years than we had in two hundred before that. An' I'm not jus' talkin' about here in th' States, either. It's a world-wide *phenomenon*." He used both hands to add quotes to the last word, grinning wryly.

"What's with the little quotes." She could feel the breath being sucked out of her chest. "Is it not really a *phenomenon*?" She copied his motion.

"No, it really isn't." He pulled his shirt off and flopped down on the sofa. "That would be somethin' unusual or unexpected. This ain't. We can predict the weather, really well I might add, an' we can see that it's changin' for th' worse at an alarming rate. Only…" He paused, watching the lines in her face grow deeper. "No one seems alarmed about it. Except the pockets o' people…like the ones at The Ranch."

"What do you mean?" Her voice dropped as she sank down on the cushion next to him. "You don't think people care about it? I know for a fact that isn't true! There's been a great deal of environmental actions taken in the last few years."

"Yeah, there's been some action, little bit, but not as much as you think. I mean, does it look like they care?" He indicated the room around them with an open palm. "For the most part, people haven't changed, an' the ones that have get a bad rap. You say it yourself every time you call th' community down south a bunch o' crazies. We get horrible, derogatory names like *tree huggers* or *activists*…an' *survivalists*."

He paused, drawing a soothing breath. "You act like preparin' for th' worst is a bad idea, but then you seem really bothered by the earthquakes an' th' hurricanes an'…everything." He lowered his tone, not intending to belittle her. "I'm sorry, little bit, but I grew up out there."

He stared into her wide green orbs. "An' for a long time, I didn' believe it either. I guess I didn't really wanna believe it. Most people don't. I know you think they're doin' what they can, with the protesters an' FEMA an' shit like that, but it's like puttin' a bandaid on a broken arm. It's not nearly enough." He paused, clenching his fists nervously for a moment. "When I see what's happenin' around us, I realize...eventually I'm gonna go home."

Her eyes grew misty. "Does that mean you're not going to help me get Jess and Jase back?"

"No, it doesn't mean that. I said that I would, an' I will. If I have t' sneak in there an' steal 'em back for you." He reached over, patting her affectionately on the knee. "You're gonna get your little brothers back, Bailey. That's a straight up promise."

"Ok." She smiled for an instant before it slipped away. "So what is it you're not telling me?"

Caleb swallowed hard, torn between the life he had always known and the girl he had come to care so much about. "I don' wanna hurt you."

She stared at him for a full minute, her tongue sliding across her teeth and making a slow lap around the inside of her mouth. She considered his words, her gut twisting into an anxious knot. "Well," she huffed, "I'm glad that you don't. What has that got to do with anything?"

"I'm afraid that lettin' you take the boys an' leave would be th' thing that gets you hurt…or killed," he finished weakly. "I tried to tell my dad, before I brought you back here…" He swallowed again, causing his Adam's apple to slide up and down. "I think you belong with us."

Leaping up from her seat, Bailey looked as if she had been slapped. "I don't want to talk about this anymore!" Bending over to grab her shoes, she stood up to find him next to her, catching her and peering down into her pure green eyes.

"I won't say anything else about it," he panted noisily. "I know it bothers you t' think about, an' I'm sorry that it does. You're still my best friend, an' I really don' wanna see anything happen t' you."

"Why couldn't we make our own place?" she suggested loudly. "If you really think they're right, we could locate a place and make our own community, only not filled with crazy people who want to hurt everyone else!"

"Stop it!" he commanded. "They don't wanna hurt people. They jus' wanna protect what they've worked for all their lives. An' that's somethin' t' think about. Maybe we could find a place t' build a similar set up," he allowed her the dream, fairly certain there wouldn't be enough time. *Not now, with things spiraling as they have been.*

"You have to finish school, little bit. Worry about that, at least for the time bein', an' I'm sorry I made you worry about the rest o' this." He swung his arm, again indicating their home and the world beyond. "This's one o' those things I shoulda kept safe for you...until you were ready t' know it."

"Yes." She stared up at him, still angry that he didn't trust her. "No worries. I'll go to bed...and sleep on it." Pulling herself out of his grasp, she made her way down the hall, closing her door behind her.

TEN

Thanks Be Given

BAILEY SLOWLY CLIMBED the steps to the apartment sooner than normal due to the early release. Thanksgiving break was upon them, and she found herself trapped in the idea of holidays and the past. She had been torn between angry and sad at their current situation for weeks, and facing the memories of what she had lost seemed only to drive her further into her depression.

Back home, their maid would be preparing a huge feast. Her grandparents would be coming down from Peoria for a visit, and it would be a day-long event. First, there would be the parades on the television; the family had a set in the den that put the one Uncle Pete had purchased to shame. *Then the giant meal followed by naps and football games to round everything out.*

Making her way into the boys' room to fire up the computer, she recalled how excited they had been each year, eager to watch the floats on the giant screen. Of course, Bailey had never really had time for her younger siblings before their lives were changed. Back then, she had no time for anyone except herself.

The girl had been seven when the twins came along, and what little time her mother had had for her before that had evaporated entirely when they were born. That's when she had started building her shell, becoming the perfect little girl in everyone's eyes. As long as they didn't look too deeply, no one would ever discover how empty she had been on the inside. *Empty and alone.*

Heaving a deep sigh, she pulled up her Facebook page. She dreaded it more and more as the days crept by, hating to see all the posts that Amanda made regarding her pending birth and marriage to Caleb. *He says it's not going to happen, but I bet it does.*

He continued to insist that Amanda and he were not a couple. But at the same time, he insisted that Bailey was only a friend, as well. *I think he has real commitment issues,* she half kidded with herself, emitting a small chuckle. The thought of him marrying the blonde only made her angrier, more despondent that his perceived deceitfulness would hold true.

Of course, there were a few pleasures that came from visiting her page. Besides her new circle of friends and their never-ending discussions, the boys would check in with her regularly. Almost daily, they sent her messages and uploaded pics of themselves, along with what went on at The Ranch, and that seemed to balance things out.

Today, they had been riding four-wheelers and had over a dozen shots for her to view. Laying her fingers across their eager faces, a cloud of sadness settled over her. *They don't even know they're in danger.*

An instant later, she shuddered, fighting the urge to cry. *They're only in danger because of you.* If she hadn't run away, they would be perfectly safe. *Of course, they wouldn't ever be allowed to leave there.* The boys had been absorbed by the clan and were living the only life they would ever know. *Unless I can get them away.*

Hearing a commotion in the front room, the girl reluctantly closed her page and shut down the machine. Exiting the hallway, she discovered her roommate bringing in a large number of bags, shocking her that he had managed to fit them all into the compartments on his bike.

"What the hell is all this?" she demanded, indicating the haul with an open palm.

Looking up at her from his bent position, Caleb grinned. "Uh… it's a surprise." He could see she didn't look pleased, but he hoped he could remove the frown she almost constantly wore, if only for a few hours, with the feast.

Bailey lifted one of the items, still in the sack. The giant turkey unmistakable by the shape, she frowned at it. "You realize I have no idea how to cook this," she berated him in a hushed voice.

"It's pre-cooked," he replied, keeping his tone low, "an' there's directions on the package on how t' heat it up. Plus, I got some other stuff that goes with it."

He lifted a few of the bags and made his way into the kitchen. "My boss gave me a ham too, so I'm gonna put it in the freezer, an' we can cook it after the turkey's gone. We should be able t' eat for a few weeks on this stuff," he ended his explanation by retrieving the remainder of the bags.

Following, still examining the bird, she cast her eyes over his purchases. "This's a lot of food for only the two of us."

"Yeah, but we can freeze part of it t' make it last longer. Plus, it'll be nice for us t' keep some traditions. Or start some new ones." He smiled again, still aware of her tension.

Shoving the creature into the fridge, Bailey turned and exited the small space, leaving him to put the remaining items away. "Amanda posted another picture of her belly. That girl is getting huge," she made the comment, only half expecting a response. "So I guess she's really pregnant. The boys are doing great. They rode four-wheelers today."

"Yeah, I saw it while I was in line at the store. H-E-B was packed," he informed her, ignoring her remark about his ex-girlfriend. "I had t' wait in line almost an hour t' check out."

"You didn't go to Wal-mart?" she queried, switching on the news.

"Oh, hell no. That place woulda been even worse." Finished

with the unpacking, he grabbed a bottle of water to join her on the couch. "Anyways, I'm off until Monday. A four-day weekend. Woohoo."

"I'm not. I work every night, not counting tomorrow." She frowned at the screen. "Have you seen this?"

"It happens every year." He watched the flickering story while flopping down on his end. "I'm surprised you never heard of it. What's th' death toll at?"

"They haven't said. We used to get the flu shot every year when mom was alive—religiously. Of course, where we lived, it was already cold by now, not still sixty degrees outside." She sighed.

"You can still get one if you want," he tried to appease her. "But it's not guaranteed. I really think these rogue viruses are gettin' more common, an' there's not really any point in vaccinations. Hell, they may even be makin' it worse, with people thinkin' they're immune only t' find out they're not."

"It's depressing." She switched the channel.

"Yeah, well, it is what it is." The blond stood to go change clothes. "I'm headin' t' the gym."

"Me, too," she agreed, moving to put on her own shorts and tank as well.

Taking her place on the treadmill next to his, she queried, "How do you know this isn't a pandemic? Or the start of one?"

Caleb shrugged, setting his machine. "I don't. But every year, the death toll is something like thirty or forty thousand in the US alone."

"Wow," she breathed. "That's a lot of people."

"Not in the big scheme o' things," he countered evenly. "It's fine, little bit. Really. I don't want you to be worried about this," he stated firmly, having noticed her increased amounts of hand washing. "That giant bottle o' hand sanitizer you added t' that suitcase you carry will protect you."

From the corner of her eye, she could see his ear to ear grin and wondered if it was the cleanser or her bag that had caused it. "Well, I hope so. I can't save the boys if something happens to me," she finished with an exaggerated sigh.

"Well"—he continued to smirk—"I tol' you to leave all o' this end o' the world business to me. I'll let you know when it's serious enough t' worry about."

Staring straight ahead, her mood did not improve. *Yeah, you keep saying that, but it's getting hard to do when there's never any good news to be had.*

Bailey awoke the following morning in a foul mood. She had read the directions for cooking the turkey the night before and had discovered that it would, in fact, be exceedingly simple. *But that's not the point*, she told herself angrily. Putting the hefty pan in the oven, it would take several hours to bake. Setting up a few of the other items, she continued to seethe over his attitude.

It bothered her that he wanted to pretend like the world was spinning on as normal. *But everything is not normal. I can feel it.* However, verbal confrontations with him got her nowhere, so she saw little point in continuing the debate.

The dishes set, she accompanied him to the gym for her daily lesson, where she took out some of her anger on him by more physical means, punching him as hard as she could when she attacked him. Once that had been completed, they ambled back to the apartment, the sun already up and the temperature nearly fifty. "You don't find this strange?" she mumbled as they climbed the stairs.

"What's strange?" He grinned, pretty sure she referred to the weather.

"It's supposed to be cold," she stated matter-of-factly.

"Naw, it'll be even warmer than this down south. The boys'll be out playing an' riding horses an' who knows what all. Snow," he considered for a brief moment, "I think I've seen maybe twice in my whole life down at The Ranch." He could tell she missed Illinois and wished he could do something to make her feel more comfortable.

Settling into a kitchen chair after his shower, he watched as she prepared the rest of their meal. "You really have turned out to be a fantastic cook," he complimented, offering her an olive branch.

"Yes," she agreed absently, noting his bare chest while continuing to go through the process of putting the green beans and potatoes on the stove. "I actually enjoy it. Like you said, it's different eating a meal that I made. More satisfying, I guess you could say," and a small smile teased her lips.

Finished with the necessities at the moment, she sighed, picking up on his efforts to make amends. Deciding to play along, she suggested quietly, "Would you like coffee or cocoa?"

"Sure." He grinned. "Whatever you feel like, I'll take some, too."

Putting on a pan of milk, she brought it to a boil and cut off the burner. Then she took out two mugs, mixing the dark liquid and adding a few marshmallows. Caleb studied her. "Someday you're gonna make a super mom. Did yours teach you t' do that?"

"No." She shook her head. "Nanna did. Or the maid...but hers wasn't the same. My mother didn't really have time for us."

"That's too bad." The blond shook his head. "My mom always liked doin' little things like this for us." He stabbed at the white goo. "And she liked you, I think."

The girl sucked in a deep breath. "I'd really rather not talk about the people at The Ranch. They wanted to kill me, remember?"

"Not all of them, little bit. An' besides, it wasn't outta malice or anything like that. They wanted t' protect their lives, their hard work. That's all. Wasn't anything against you." He sighed. *Damn. That's exactly what I wanted to avoid.*

"Well, assuming I would give them away or do anything to hurt them was wrong, no matter what their excuse."

"Yes, it was," he agreed, taking a sip of the hot liquid. "An' given time, I think they woulda seen that they could trust you. If you hadn't needed t' finish school here, you woulda had time t' show 'em."

"Hmmp," she grunted, flicking on the set to discover the parade broadcast. The sight brought another small flicker of a smile. "We used to watch these. It was one of the few things we did as a family."

"Oh yeah?" He grinned. "I like traditions. They help bind us to our families an' friends. We used t' gather aroun' at th' diner for a huge meal. An' each of us'd stand up an' tell one thing we were thankful for. Everyone did it, no matter how young."

"And what are you thankful for, Caleb?" She glared at him, expecting something that would undoubtedly piss her off.

"I'm thankful I met you." His blue eyes stared into her soft green orbs. "I know you prolly find it hard t' believe," he sighed, allowing his focus to flitter away, "but you're a much better friend t' me than anyone else ever has been."

Her eyes narrowed, and she couldn't resist the urge to push for a fight. "I bet your bride to be would be so brokenhearted to hear that."

He busted out with a loud laugh. "Well, my bride t' be will be in for a shock when I get that whole situation straightened out. I'm gonna make her get tested, an' then I'll have proof that th' kid ain' mine. An' besides, I tol' you I'm not marryin' her." He rubbed the outside of his lips for a moment, studying the girl across from him. "I wonder who the father is," he finally admitted in a soft tone.

A jolt of electricity shot through her as Bailey recalled the night they had heard a couple going at it in the barn. "You don't think that was her, do you?" she spoke of the event, assuming he would know what she referred to.

"I dunno." He shrugged. "All I know is it's gonna be a huge mess when the shit finally hits the fan." He grinned again, feeling a twinge of joy that she had finally reached a point of at least considering he could be telling the truth. *Now that's something I'm really thankful for.*

ELEVEN

Naughty or Nice

ALISSA PORTER STARED at her post, a small smile curling her lips. *Well, it's about time, Bailey.* She had promised the *menfolk* three months ago that she would help make the girl feel welcome in their little tight-knit community, but for the first time since, there had been a sign it might actually be working.

Sitting up straighter in her chair, she quickly typed out her reply to the girl's comment. Her hand poised above the mouse, she read it again. *Yeah, that's exactly what I wanna say.* Satisfied, she hit the enter key, sending her message across cyberspace, sending her words to the girl she genuinely hoped would one day be her neighbor and friend.

On the other end, Bailey stared at the screen, catching herself giggling along. Typing her own opinion, she continued to smile, noting how some of the other girls had joined in. *Wow, this is nice.* She caught a brief fit of laughter, her mind dragging up her old division for The Ranch members: naughty or nice. *Yeah, you girls are all on the nice list. Trust me.*

Bailey had once thought of Facebook and her web of friends as the center of her universe. Surprising herself, she had almost found it cathartic the day she had pitched them to the wind, cleansing her life of the people who surrounded her but knew nothing about her inner being.

In the weeks that followed, she had spied on the new friends on her list, strangely attracted to the people who held her brothers in their grasp—the group who had wanted her dead. The girl had gathered intel on the entire community, pouring over their profiles and seeing them in a new light.

It saddened her after Amanda made her announcement, aware that the naughty list held far more names. It bothered her seeing her posts and the way the others responded to them. After the initial push, Bailey stopped visiting those pages, having gleaned all that she needed to know about them.

Choosing to visit the pages of the smaller group, the few Bailey considered to be her allies on the nice list, she spent time each week getting to know them little by little. Amazingly, once she started to dig, she discovered this small group of women appeared ready, if not eager, to accept her as one of them.

Alissa had reached out to the girl when she had physically been in their midst. Being a few hundred miles away might have put a damp-ener on her efforts if it had not been for the ease of clicking a few buttons. Tagging her new auburn-haired friend, the youngest Fox daughter included Bailey in a few posts and discussions about food, recipes, and the like. Soon, it seemed as if the solid brick wall that protected the clan still extended around the other girl as well, holding her there in spirit.

At first, Bailey felt wary of their friendship, only interacting with them out of being polite and keeping her eye on them at the same time. She read much but commented little. Soon, however, the nice list had grown, including Alissa's daughters, Judy and Lynnette. The pair of them had moved to The Ranch at around the age that the twins had joined the lot, so they had memories of the outside world as well.

With the altered dynamic, the younger trio delved deeply into debates over music and movies, and before they knew it, Amber and Rebecca Burns were a part of their small circle. Their discussions branched to include all sorts of interesting topics, and today's post was the one Alissa had been waiting for, the one that made it obvious Bailey viewed the group as her friends.

Flipping over to her list of contacts, she sent a private message to Peter, adding a link to the post: *I think your Bailey will return to us. I gave my word that I would help, but please be sure I haven't been an instrument in her destruction. I don't know if I could live with myself if that were to happen.*

A few days later, Pete sent his reply: *No guarantees. She still has enemies here, so we will wait. Keep up the good work; it is appreciated. Bailey needs our friendship and love, either way.*

Alissa stared at the response for a long time. She had liked the girl from the beginning, fully understanding what it was like to join the community after having lived and loved life on the outside of it. Putting her reservations aside, she continued to share their beliefs— about the world and what would become of it.

TWELVE

If They're Right

BAILEY CROSSED THE STREET, rubbing her hands together to warm them. She had finally taken to wearing her jacket, as the temperatures were beginning to qualify as cooler. Smiling slightly at the giant Santa scene that covered the glass at the shop, she made her way inside.

"Hey, Mark," she called as she passed him. Heading to the back, she shoved her bag in the locker to begin her shift. To her surprise, he followed her into the smaller room. "Is something wrong?" she queried.

"Nope. You are an exceptional employee. I realize you're graduating in a few months and probably headin' off to college after that," he made the suggestion, pausing to see if she would fill in the details, but she had always been a private person, not sharing much of anything about herself—past, present, or future.

When she failed to reply, he became blunt. "I need a new shift manager, an' I was hoping you would take the spot. There's a nice little raise that goes along with that, by the way," he tacked on the incentive, hoping it would entice her.

"Mark"—she sighed—"I appreciate the offer, but I really can't put any more on my plate." He wasn't aware of the turmoil that lurked in the back of her mind on a daily basis—no one was. There would be no way she could make room for anything else, even if it meant more pay.

Checking her reflection in the mirror, she dismissed him, leaving him standing in the office, gaping after her. Arriving at her register, she swiped her card and began taking orders.

In between customers, she flipped the lobby television to CNN, which had become her norm. She couldn't hear, since the sound had been muted, but she could see the text at the bottom from the captioning and had been following the latest flu outbreak for days. Her mind never far from The Ranch as of late, she recalled Alissa's latest post, considering, *What if they're right?*

Taking her break, she had just taken a bite of her cheeseburger when Caleb slid into the booth next to her, playfully pinning her in. "Hey, little bit."

"Hey, Caleb." She shot him a quick grin, then returned to eating her meal.

Adjusting to pull off his coat, he indicated the screen they faced. "Pretty crazy, huh? Eighteen more people died today in Boston. Who knows how many everywhere else? This's the worst year yet, an' it's not even close to over."

"Yeah," she agreed between chews, finishing the burger and starting on the fries. "It doesn't sound like many when you hear about those pockets, but the totals…" She paused, emitting a small shudder. "It's kinda creepy how the bodies seem to be piling up."

"Yup." Her roommate accepted the tray from her co-worker and began to unwrap his meal. "You need t' go back yet?"

"Naw. I still have like six minutes." Her eyes remained glued to the screen. "Seventy-eight people in the last three days in Washington State. That's both ends of the country." She shook her head slowly, side to side. "I don't like this."

"Would you mind if I got you a gift?" he changed the subject abruptly. "You know, for Christmas?"

Her head turned as if in slow motion, looking at him squarely. "Do you want one in return?"

Giving her a chuckle, he shook his head. "Not really, I jus' had somethin' picked out for you. Somethin' you might like."

"Scoot over." She tapped him on the arm with the back of her hand, indicating for him to stand. "I don't care if you do." She made it to her feet. "But I can't guarantee I'll get you anything." She frowned down at him when he sat. "You should have said something sooner, while I still had time to shop."

"Naw, save your money." He waved a fry at her. "It's not a big deal."

"Mmhmm…" She grimaced, returning to her register while pondering his offer. In the end, she had grown accustomed to his off and on behavior and the way he seemed to oscillate between their relationship qualifying as a friendship…or something more. *Today we must be on the more side,* she considered with a tiny grin.

Caleb remained at the shop, relaxing in the booth and watching the broadcast. *She's right. This's crazy.* He shook his head at the scene. The number scrolled across the bottom. *Death toll reaches thirty-two thousand.* "Wow," he whispered out loud. "That's a lot for only this far along." *Still, it's not a pandemic…at least not yet.*

Walking together after she had clocked out, Bailey thought about his request and his odd behavior. He had finished his studies right after the Thanksgiving holiday. However, he continued to come to the store and escort her home in the evenings, and that put her on edge.

"You don't think anything would happen to me, do you?"

Her question caught him off guard. "Whadda ya mean?"

"Well, you come over and walk me home every night, even though you don't have to. If something was wrong, you'd tell me, wouldn't you?" Her mind flashed briefly to the Facebook pages she seldom pulled up anymore and wondered if there had been any more threats from down south.

"Naw." He shook his head as they mounted the stairs. "It's a habit I guess. I'll stop if it bothers you."

"I didn't say it bothered me," she countered evenly, turning down the hall and calling over her shoulder, "Goodnight, Caleb."

"Goodnight, little bit." He allowed her to retreat, aware that she did so less often in the weeks since the last holiday, a sure sign her faith in him had become secured. He still feared she read more into their relationship than he was prepared to admit, but that, too, seemed to be leveling out.

Reaching for the remote, he pulled up the program he had been watching back at the shop. Removing his shirt and shoes, he stretched out in Pete's favorite spot. A short time later, he noticed that she stood in the hallway, viewing the program from over his shoulder.

"You afraid to sit on the couch with me?" he teased.

Stepping more into the light, "No," she retorted. "I can't sleep. You still watching this?" She observed that he qualified as half naked, the same as Pete often did. *Must be a man thing.* Hiding her discomfort, she let it go, as she always did.

"Yeah, they're talkin' about why the flu vaccine ain't been workin' right for th' last few years, makin' the casualty numbers go up. It's pretty interesting hearin' all th' science behind it."

"If you say so." She curled up in the bend of the sectional, putting her feet up in the middle area between them. "I think it's creepy. You know, Alissa told me that people dying from a massive disease was one way they thought the world was going to end."

"Yeah," he agreed, reaching over to massage her foot. "There's lot'sa theories. An' that one is pretty popular." He wafted a hand at the screen.

"You want an ice age," she teased, kicking at him slightly, enjoying the rub and the way his muscles moved in his chest when he did it.

"I don' want anything." He looked over at her, pressing the back of his head deeper into the cushion behind him. "But it don' hurt t' be prepared."

She stared at him, having been weeks since they had talked about The Ranch in earnest. "I still think those people are crazy."

"Yeah, they are, the crazy part being if they turn out t' be right." He played his hand tight, aware of the posts she had been taking part in. *She's becoming drawn to them whether she realizes it or not.*

Bailey grunted, having thought the same thing too many times recently to count. "You think this's a sign?" Her eyes darted over at the flickering screen.

"I think"—he paused, changing to the other foot—"that there really isn't a single thing that could destroy us. There's too many of us humans, an' we're too widely adapted. Pockets o' people would hang on, no matter what or how devastating the event. But that's only useful if you're in one o' those pockets."

"Well, you know, the dinosaurs hung on for a while too, but they're not here anymore," she toyed with a tiny grin.

"Some of 'em are." He chuckled. "An' that's not what I mean. Le's say another asteroid did hit the earth. Whatever catastrophe followed"—he paused, pressing between her toes—"would be nothing compared t' what men would do t' each other in the panic. That would be the real disaster—the fight for survival."

"You said that before, that man was the greatest threat." Her lip curled into a slight pout at the idea of man versus man. "I think people would want to help each other."

He stared into her clear green eyes, lost in thought for a moment. "I don' think we have anything t' worry about," he reassured her. "One little event, like this plague thing, won' be enough t' cause any panics." Giving her a slow grin, he noticed the program had come to an end. "You're on Christmas break, right?"

"Yeah," she conceded, finally feeling sleep creeping up on her. "My last final exam was Friday."

"I'm gonna call in tomorrow an' take you t' do somethin' different."

"Like what?" She snuggled deeper into the couch, his touch relaxing her more by the minute.

"I dunno." He shrugged. "There's gotta be somethin' around here t' do." In the next instant, the idea sprang to mind. "I got it. I'll take you on an adventure—a surprise one…in Odessa," he beamed.

Pulling her foot away, she giggled, not bothering to argue. "Whatever. I'm going to bed," and she made her way to her room, closing the door behind her.

Cutting off the set, he followed her down the hall, eager to get some rest himself. Stretching out on Pete's oversized mattress, he stared at the ceiling, recalling how she had slowly been coming around. Drifting off to dream, he hoped she would enjoy his surprise and the warming trend, with the girl at least, would continue.

THIRTEEN

A Christmas Story

THE NEXT MORNING, Bailey appeared to have taken to the idea of an adventure. "Odessa's not far away, is it?" she asked on their trek to the gym.

"Yeah. It's about twenty miles. We'll need t' bundle up, 'cause it gets a little chilly on the bike"—he nodded—"but it's close enough. It's crowded too, so we're goin' early enough t' beat th' crowd. Hopefully, most people'll be shopping, an' that's not what we're gonna do."

Going through her training, the girl continued to hold a pleased expression and pressed for more while they walked back to change and prepare for the day. "You're not going to give me a clue about what you've got planned?" she cajoled him with pleading green orbs. She emitted a tiny tinkle of a giggle when she caught his eye.

"Nope." He joined in with a hearty laugh. "It wouldn' be a surprise if I did!"

After their showers, Bailey cooked a good breakfast for them, and Caleb made a call to his boss to inform him that he wasn't going in. Finally, the pair dressed warmly and huddled on his bike for the longer trip to the neighboring town. She curled behind him to help block the wind, and she felt fortunate the community they headed towards lay west, as the rising sun felt good on her back as they rode.

Arriving at the mall, he was forced to reveal his surprise when they discovered that the skating rink didn't open to the public until ten. "Sorry, little bit. Looks like we got over an hour t' kill."

Her smile remaining, she stood next to the glass, peering at the ice rink filled with a wide expanse of the glossy substance. "Jesus, Caleb, what makes you think I can skate?"

"I dunno." He grinned, leaning a shoulder against the clear wall so that he faced her. "If you can't, we can learn together."

Making their way to the restaurant down the way, they ordered a couple of warm drinks and shared a small amount of conversation. On the inside, Bailey's spirits soared at the prospect of going skating. Growing curious at her quiet demeanor, he prodded, "Ok, so was this not a good surprise, or was it?"

Grinning, she nodded, "It's a good one," and she opened up to him, describing more of her past for him than she ever had before while they waited. Sticking to the parts that made her happy about her childhood, she took care to avoid the memories that didn't. "You know I grew up in Illinois, so I've actually been on many skating adventures. I guess you could say I really like the cold weather. It's not like this area, either." She wafted a hand around before returning her fingers to the warm cup. "There's actual trees and grass, and you can't see all over creation because the land has a bit more contour."

Caleb took a noisy sip of coffee while he listened without interrupting. He had seen her home and where her family lived, but since his presence there had been for nefarious purposes, he felt glad that she had forgotten.

"Back home, by this point," she continued with a grin, "we would have several inches of snow on the ground, and winter would be in full swing—building snowmen, sledding, you name it." Watching him while she tasted her hot chocolate, the thought occurred to her how the term *back home* didn't creep into her conversations nearly as often as it used to.

She felt a little sad at the idea, that she no longer missed the place that she grew up. *Things change,* she told herself with a small smile, *and people change.* Suppressing a wider grin, she could admit for the first time that Caleb had made it back to the top of the nice list and had regained the title of her best friend.

Taking to the ice after the rink opened, the couple glided around the oval, whereupon the young man discovered his female companion qualified as quite skilled with a pair of blades, at least the kind you would find on the bottom of ice skates. Leaving him after a few minutes, she zipped past him, picking up speed and performing several spins and leaps.

Stopping next to him when he finally gave up and leaned against a wall, she grinned from ear to ear. "What's the matter? You're not enjoying this?"

"Oh, I am," he assured her, the look on her face worth twice what the activity had cost him, maybe more. "Go on. You're really good at this. I'll just hang out over here an' watch."

Pushing away, Bailey continued to fly past him, working her way through her repertoire of moves. Smiling brightly the entire time, she felt a joy she hadn't come close to in nearly a year. Reluctantly removing her footwear a short time later, she clasped his arm, wanting him to look at her when she thanked him.

"I mean it." She nodded eagerly. "This was the best present you could have given me. I'm so happy I could kiss you!"

"Well, thanks," he shared in her excitement, displaying his full set of perfect teeth, "but this was just a little day out. Your present's at home. I'll give it to you when we get back…and I will definitely pass on the kiss, little bit."

"Oh," she exclaimed in surprise. "Well, it's not Christmas yet! And I was only kidding about the kiss."

"Haha, very funny. But it is Christmas Eve." He shrugged. "It's close enough for you to get your gift."

Placing their boots on the counter, the pair snaked through the crowd that had pressed their way into the mall while they played. "Yuck," she muttered under her breath, thoughts of the flu epidemic leaping to the front of her mind.

"Don't worry." He clamped on to her shoulder, steering her through the horde. "I don' think any o' them are contagious."

She laughed that he had read her thoughts, pushing to the exit and thankful to be out of the cramped space. "Let's go home." She sighed, and he didn't waste any time getting her there.

Clomping up the stairs, they entered the apartment, shaking out of their coats and hanging them on the small row of hooks she had placed behind the door. Heading into the kitchen to warm milk for cocoa, she grinned between rosy cheeks when he handed her the small flat box. "Wow, this is heavy." Pulling at the ribbon, she quickly removed the paper, then lifted the lid, and breathed, "Oh my God!" Staring at the shiny pistol, she could not believe her eyes.

Her gaze darting up to meet his, he smiled. "Merry Christmas."

"Thanks," she placed the carton on the counter. "Merry Christmas to you, too. And thank you for this." She indicated her new treasure. "Are you going to teach me how to shoot it?"

"Yeah." He nodded, toying with the ribbon. "I got us a membership at a local gun club. I've been buying ammo every week. It's rationed, so I knew it would take me a while to build a stockpile."

Dropping the clip, she inspected it, recalling what she had learned about them from his books and her trip to Academy several weeks before. "Thank you, Caleb," she mumbled, genuinely grateful for the gift. "This really means a lot to me."

"You're very welcome, little bit," he replied softly, as it meant a lot to him, too.

FOURTEEN

Little Voices

BAILEY AWOKE FEELING SOMEWHAT forlorn on Christmas morning. The crisp air met her at the door when she left the apartment to go to the gym, but no snow had fallen in the west Texas town. Caleb at her side, they made their way across the compound for her morning training, then returned to their dwelling, where they would finally enjoy the ham that he had brought home for Thanksgiving.

It only cheered her a little when she prepared their meal, and Caleb could sense her sadness as she moved about the tiny kitchen. While she did so, he slipped into the other room to use the computer, sending her uncle a short message, inquiring how things were going and asking if there would be any chance she could speak to the boys some time that day.

Leaning on his elbows for a few minutes, staring at the text, he wasn't sure if the man would even respond. Since the couple had asked to be left alone, they rarely had direct contact from any of the group members. He knew that Bailey still checked in a few times a week, but he could tell seeing Amanda's posts bothered her. *I can't believe she actually thinks she's going to get away with this,* he thought of the tall blonde with a degree of disgust.

Flipping over to his parents' pages, he posted a greeting to each of them on their walls, wishing them a happy holiday. Finally, he sent a message to Bailey herself, telling her how glad he was that he had such a dear friend to share his holiday with. Again, he had no idea if or when she would see it, but since it was the thought that counts, he felt satisfied with his effort.

Shutting down the machine, he returned to the table to sip on hot apple cider and watch while she put herself into her work. Deciding he didn't want to wait, he went to find her phone. Opening it to his message, he slid it across the counter while hiding around the end in a playful manner.

Stopping with her hands suspended above the bowl before her, her gaze moved over to the android he pushed a little at a time towards her. "What are you doing?" she demanded, her words gruff.

"I'm...showing you something." He grinned sheepishly, noting her dark tone. When she didn't move, he teased, "Come on, Bailey. You can do it."

Noting he used her actual name, she lifted her face to look at him, her auburn locks falling to the side. "What is it?"

"Just a little message I sent you." He shrugged, still beaming.

Wiping her hands, she reached for the device. Relighting the screen and reading it, her lips moved slightly as her mind formed the words. Reaching the end, her eyes grew misty. "Wow, that's pretty strong, don't you think?"

"Not really." He nodded, holding his smile in place. "I mean it. You're my best friend, little bit. You have been for a while. It's about time I said so."

"Thanks, Caleb. You're my best friend, too." Clearing the counter, she slid her arms around his neck, allowing him to squeeze her and noting that afterwards, she felt calmer. "You want anything special for today?" she asked in a meek little voice.

"Only a smile." He traced the underside of her chin with a finger, eliciting a curl on her lips.

Reaching up, she brushed his hand away, returning to her bowl. Her mouth remained in a small scoop, her heart pounding in her chest. "You want to put on some Christmas music?"

"From…where?" he queried.

"Look some up in my phone. I'm sure there has to be some out there somewhere." She indicated the cell with an extended pinky.

A few minutes later, she had finished with everything for the moment, and all her dishes were on their own for a while. Moving towards her roommate, a larger smile spread across her lips. "Any chance you know how to dance?"

"Any chance?" He snickered. "I was the only guy with six girls my age. There was no way I coulda gone without learnin'." Turning, he shoved the table and chairs against the balcony door, expanding the space. Offering his hands, she slipped into his arms, and they turned a small circle in the end of the kitchen.

When the song ended, she looked up into his soft blue eyes. "Thank you, Caleb," she breathed. "You are a very dear friend to me as well." For a brief instant, she wondered if he might kiss her, fairly certain that he wouldn't, when her phone began to chime. Reaching to grab it, she answered, somewhat disappointed at the interruption. "Hello?"

"Hi, sis!" her brothers called in unison, obviously on speaker together.

Her face breaking into a wide grin, the girl shrieked, "Oh my God! Merry Christmas, guys!" Elated to hear from them, she placed her phone on conference and laid it on the table so that their little voices could fill the room. "Did you guys have a good morning?"

"We sure did!" Jess practically shouted. "We was hopin' you'd come to see us, but Uncle Pete says you're too busy right now."

"Yeah," Jase agreed over the top of him. "So when you get un-busy, then you need to come home, Bailey!"

Home? The word instantly struck a nerve. *So The Ranch is home now.* She bit her quivering bottom lip, aware for the first time that her brothers might not want to leave The Ranch even if she were able to free them. "I'm so glad to hear from you," she said, hoping to cover her pain.

Not fooled, Caleb raised his hand, allowing it to run gently down her back while the boys filled her in about the new pony.

"It was born just a few days ago," Jase explained, "but it can already walk. We named him Star 'cause he's all black with a white place on his head, right between the eyes."

"Yeah," Jess joined in. "An' John says he's our horse, too. We get to keep it and brush it and do everything for it!"

"Wow, you guys, that's so great!" She recalled watching the man next to her care for the horses not so long ago. Giving him a sideways glance, she forced a small smile, sliding her arm around him for an embrace.

Stroking her hair, Caleb wasn't sure if asking for the call had been a good idea or not. *Yeah, she's in a hard place,* he admitted to himself. *Hopefully she'll find where she belongs.* Giving her a squeeze, he continued to grin while he listened.

A few minutes later, the banter winding down, he called softly into the device, "Hey, guys, is your Uncle Pete around there anywhere?"

"Yeah, I'm here," the older man spoke up for the first time.

"Hey, man"—he paused for a moment, staring down into the large green pools of happiness—"thanks for the phone call."

"Don't mention it." Peter's smile came through loud and clear. "Looking forward to you two making it home. Say goodbye, boys," he instructed, and the twins began calling their farewells loudly.

"See you soon, boys," Bailey said hers as well, ending the connection with a small sigh. "You asked him to call me, didn't you?" she accused in a soft voice.

"I suggested it," he admitted quietly. "I thought it might make you feel better."

Giving him a long stare, she could feel a knot in the pit of her stomach. "I really appreciate that, Caleb." She drew in a deep breath, aware that she had been drawn in. "Please don't hurt me again. I really hope that I can trust you and that you're right about this whole…thing…with Amanda."

"I'm right," he professed without hesitation. "There's no way that I'm wrong."

Nodding, she turned away, returning to their meal, determined to enjoy the rest of their day the very best that she could. She opened the oven to pull out the ham while thinking, *I almost wish we* had *made the trip to The Ranch.*

FIFTEEN

Ice Age

CALEB RETURNED to work the day after Christmas, and Bailey went into the shop, feeling a little happier than she had since their arrival in Midland. She still felt the need to train, but the idea that her brothers would never want to leave their new family and friends had taken her thoughts and ideas in a new direction.

When Caleb came into the store, she went on her break and picked up her dinner, taking the seat across from him and demanding quickly, "Do you think that the ones at The Ranch who didn't want me there would ever change their minds?"

His jaw dropped slightly, he considered his words carefully. "Well, little bit, it's really hard t' say. For one, I'm not even sure who exactly didn' want you there. An' for the other"—he frowned—"why would you ask?"

"I don't know," she lied flatly, taking a bite out of a chicken strip, then dipping it in the gravy with a thoughtful expression. "I think that the boys may not want to leave The Ranch," she finally fessed up. "They seem really happy there. And not just on the phone yesterday. On Facebook, they are always smiling in their pictures—"

"Now, wait." Caleb held up a hand. "I don't wanna burst your bubble, but you need t' have a clear understanding o' the situation. You know your uncle posts that stuff, so yeah, he's not gonna post anything that don't fit with his agenda."

Stopping in mid chew, she gaped at him. "His agenda? What's that supposed to mean?"

"Well, you've known since we got here that they wanted you t' go back there. Why, we can't be as sure about, but they have no reason t' show you th' bad side of anything. So keep that in mind when you think about what you see on Facebook. It's purely there t' draw you in. Tha's all I'm sayin'."

Continuing to eat, she gave him a long stare. "Ok, I see your point. But on the phone, they clearly sounded happy."

"Again, they jus' got a new pony, an' what kid wouldn' be happy about that?"

"Caleb, if you think something is wrong with the way they are being treated, you damn well better say so!" she bit at him, becoming angry.

Instantly sorry he had upset her, the tall blond ran his right hand roughly over his face before he tried to sidestep the issue. "I don't think that they are. I'm just sayin' if they were, it'd be impossible t' tell from here. We only see what they want us t' see, that's it." Staring up at the screen, he frowned at the map being presented above her head.

Seeing his expression, she produced a large scowl. "I thought you were going to be honest with me. How can you say one thing, but your face totally says something else, and not call it lying?"

His eyes darting to hers, then back up at the flickering display, he licked his lip anxiously. "Little bit, you need to take a deep breath"—he paused, aware that she had many friends and family still in the place she had once called home—"then scoot over here by me."

Her expression growing angry, she felt certain that he toyed with her somehow. Tossing her fry back into the pile, she grabbed one of the brown paper napkins and calmly wiped at her face and fingers.

Then, sliding out of the booth, she stood and turned around to face the screen, which read *Storm of the Century* in bold red letters. "Oh my God!"

"Bailey, sit down." He reached to catch her hand and pull her towards the bench next to him.

"Oh my God," she breathed more quietly, her voice trembling. "Why is this happening?"

"I don' know. Le's jus' watch the report, an' we'll know more about it," he tried to comfort her.

"I can't. I have to go back to work," she whined slightly.

"Then go, an' don' worry. We can't do anything at this exact moment anyways, so I'll watch an' see what all I can find out, an' I'll fill you in on th' walk home."

Glancing over at him, she slid her arms around him for a quick squeeze. "Ok. I can do that. Something else I'm trusting you to know for me until I'm ready for it." She smiled timidly at the idea.

"Yeah," he agreed. "Go on, an' I'll see you in a bit."

Rising, Bailey returned to her post for the last two hours of her shift, her eyes on the screen whenever she had a moment but unable to make heads or tails of the maps and models that flashed across the news cast. Once the store closed, she quickly took care of her register and restocking the front, asking Mark to let her out when she had finished.

Outside, Caleb waited for her, and she demanded, "Well?" as soon as the door had closed behind her.

"Le's walk," he suggested quietly, guiding her towards the light. Once they were away from the building and on their way home, he began to explain. "It hasn't happened yet, but they're sayin' it's only about twelve hours away."

"What is?" she interrupted, her anxiety getting the better of her patience. "What the hell is *the storm of the century?*"

"A giant ice storm has been sitting over Canada for a week. It's pushing down, crossing the Great Lakes, an' expected t' engulf most, if not all, o' Michigan, Wisconsin…an' Illinois. An' maybe even some o' Indiana an' Ohio." He shrugged, knowing the latter would not be the part she cared about.

"And what are they going to do about it?" Her mind recalled the conversation they had months ago, when he confessed to thinking an ice age would destroy the earth. *Or was it that it would kill a lot of people?* She couldn't remember. "Isn't this what you were telling me about, an Ice Age that would kill everyone?"

Caleb laughed loudly, climbing the stairs next to her. "This isn't an ice age, little bit. It's a storm. An' as a matter o' fact, not so unusual up north. The natural gas lines are packed, an' they can last for weeks even if we don' send 'em any more fuel."

"That's not the point," she countered angrily. "This is not normal! Yeah, it gets cold, but an actual storm? And if it's going to be bad enough they're reporting on it…" Her voice trailed away.

"They're reporting on it because people need to take precautions. They need to stock up on food an' supplies, be prepared in case it lasts more than a few days. Come on, little bit. You know th' news feeds the hype an' runs on ratings."

"Well, yes, I know that very well." She stared at him, her eyes growing wide. "But do you think my grandparents are ok?"

"Why wouldn't they be?" He shrugged. "They're in a community, aren't they? In Peoria?"

"Yes. It's a retirement village. They have a little two-bedroom condo, but I don't think the owners really do anything. It's like a group of old people, all clumped together."

Studying her features, he could tell she was overcome with the idea they could really be hurt. "Here"—he nudged her—"le's get inside, and you can call them."

"Oh my God," she breathed. "The last time I called them this late, I woke her and scared the hell out of her," Bailey recalled her desperate attempt last spring.

"Well, we can do it now or in the morning." He smoothed her hair for her. "But I don' want you losing sleep over this. I'm sure it's fine."

After a few minutes of discussion, he persuaded the girl to get some rest, and they would make the call in the morning. "I'll have to get their number from Uncle Peter," she realized at the end. "I don't have it in my new phone, and Nanna never responded to my message to give it to me."

"Ok. You go get some rest, an' we'll take care o' all that in the mornin'." After watching her disappear into her room and close the door, he went into his own to make a call.

A few minutes later, he had spoken to her uncle and had the number jotted on a notepad. Ready to end the connection, he decided to put a bug in the other man's ear and suggested in a playful tone, "Hey, wouldn' it be neat if Bailey decided she wanted t' live on Th' Ranch?"

"Whadda ya mean?" Peter asked warily.

"Well, after she got used t' bein' there, things here seem t' freak her out a little more. This whole Ice Storm up north really has her on edge, especially with flu outbreaks an' earthquakes before that. I think she may be considerin' skippin' college an' returnin' t' Th' Ranch, if you guys would have her."

Instantly, the man's voice filled with anger. "You make sure she don't choose that! She needs to finish her education, an' college comes next. If she comes back here, she may never get to it."

Taken aback by his sharp tone, Caleb rolled his tongue for a moment, then pushed the issue. "It wouldn't be 'cause they would hurt her, would it?"

"Naw, I don' think they would, not if she's here t' stay. She made some friends here over th' summer. But that's not the point! She has a chance at a better education than most people, since her grandmother put her inheritance into that fund for her," he revealed.

"What fund?" Caleb quipped, unaware of any such arrangement.

"Louise called me before Thanksgiving. Said the estate had been settled. They divided everything into fourths, putting a share into a trust for each o' the kids to go to college on, an' they get the balance when they graduate. An' a fourth for me to help pay for raising them." He sighed. "Not that I need it. Jus' give her the number, Caleb. Let her make her call an' see that they're all right. But don' let her get hung up on the idea o' comin' back here. I got the boys taken care of. She needs to worry about her own life."

Caleb ended the call, frowning at the older man's seeming oscillation about the girl's future. *One minute, he's drawing her in, the next he's pushing her away.* His mind torn between loyalty to his friends and family back home and what he felt for the one who shared his space, he prepared for the night.

Stripping down, he slipped into the oversized bed, still considering the girl who slept in the next room. Blinking into the darkness, the thought occurred to him that his life would be quite lonely if she chose to go off to college, leaving him to return to The Ranch without her.

SIXTEEN

Mob Mentality

THE FOLLOWING MORNING, Bailey leapt out of bed as soon as the alarm went off. Throwing on her shorts and tank, she pulled on a pair of sweatpants over the bottoms for warmth during the trip across the compound. Out in the hall, she could hear her roommate moving around, so she opened the door and called, "You think I should call Uncle Pete this morning or do it after we get back from the gym?"

"I already talked t' him." He waved the slip of paper at her, the number scrawled across it. Appearing in the opening, he tried to smile. "You can call her when we get back."

"What's wrong?" she probed, seeing the despondent look on his face. "Has something else happened?"

Beckoning with a slow wave of his hand, he mumbled, "I'll tell you on the way over."

Following, Bailey pulled on her jacket, and they arrived in the small room a few minutes later. Sliding out of the coat and sweats, she flopped down on the mat and began to stretch and warm up, demanding, "Ok, tell."

"Your Uncle expects you t' go t' college when you finish this year," he informed her bluntly. "They have the money set aside for you, an' it's pretty much a done deal."

"What?" She frowned at the seemingly unrelated revelation. "What has that got to do with my grandparents freezing to death?"

"Nothin'." He shrugged. "He just tol' me that last night when I talked t' him. They split up your parents' estate an' made a fund for you t' go t' college. An' you're goin'."

He didn't look at her when he spoke, and the girl had an odd feeling in her chest, as if she couldn't breathe, while watching his hunched frame bend and move. "And what if I don't want to go?"

"I don't think he's gonna give you a choice." His blue eyes darted to meet hers.

The girl exhaled loudly, feeling the anger wash over her. Getting to his feet, he pulled her up, and they began to spar. Using the rush of adrenaline, she worked her way through the moves she had been practicing for the last few weeks.

"You know, you've gotten really good at this," he praised when they were done.

"I bet," she clipped, still upset. *Men—always assuming that they're in charge of me.*

"Seriously." He grinned. "You're pretty good at breakin' holds an' defense, plus you're even pickin' up on some o' the attacks quite nicely."

"Well, I'm tired of feeling like everyone wants to control me." Her mouth curved into a heavy frown, and she glared at him, lumping him in with the rest for the moment.

"Not everyone." He grazed her chin. "An' even then, we jus' want what's best for you."

"Ok," she agreed. "So when do *I* get to decide what's best for me?"

The tall blond only shook his head, observing her muscles flexing when she redressed. *Yeah, she's filled out quite nicely.* He smirked at her form. "I bet you could give 'Manda a run for her money these days." He chuckled, forgetting that the blonde was currently pregnant.

Ignoring the presumed jab, Bailey led the way back to their apartment, where she pulled out her phone to make the call. Her grandmother seemed less than pleased to hear from the girl, as she informed her that they were both fine and well stocked for the impending event. Ending the conversation abruptly, the elderly woman left the girl feeling confused.

"Well"—she sighed—"I guess they're ok. She didn't sound very happy that I called to check on them."

"Ok." He shook his head. "Don' let it bother you. You can't do anything for them if they're not ok, an' worryin' about it ain't gonna do any good."

Bailey raised her chin to look at him. "You think something's wrong, and she doesn't want to tell me?"

"Maybe." He shrugged. "We'll keep an eye on th' weather, an' you can call again later if you want to."

"Ok." She nodded slowly, returning her gaze to the dark screen before setting it aside to make breakfast. "I guess I can."

As soon as their meal was finished, the girl took up a spot on the couch, searching their saved channels for one reporting on the storm. It turned out three of them were covering it, so she flicked between them periodically, picking up bits and pieces of the current situation and the predictions.

At one point, she caught a broadcast showing a swarm of people that had ransacked a local store in Milwaukee and then another spot of violence to the south, outside of Chicago. "Why would people go nuts like that?" She thoughtfully stared at the scene.

"Well, it's a kind o' mob mentality," Caleb explained. "People acting in a group lose their sense o' identity an' go with the flow more easily, even when they're committing crimes or doin' things they normally wouldn'. Fear an' anger feed into that, an' tha's how riots happen. Kinda like lynch mobs in the ol' west."

"Wow," the girl breathed as a camera panned across rows and rows of empty shelving. "So they went in and cleared the place out. Didn't even pay for any of it."

"Probably not," he agreed. "The thing is, there really may not've been a shortage, an' they likely even took things they didn't need. But if the crowd perceived that there was or that they were missin' out on somethin'…losin' somehow, it adds t' the commotion."

"Reminds me of Christmas shoppers. They get nuts over a stupid toy."

"Exactly." Caleb gave her a small grimace. "Then add t' that survival instincts an' the fear factor, an' you've got a real problem."

Bailey cut her eyes over, studying the man next to her. "That's what you were talking about happening here. If there ever was a real crisis, the people would be more dangerous than anything else."

"Yeah," he agreed more quietly, sorry that he had mentioned it. "Don' be afraid, little bit. I'm sure what's hapnin' up north'll smooth out once th' storm passes, an' I don't see how any o' that could reach us all the way down here."

For the next few days, Bailey anxiously kept her eye on the news, noting that everything across four states seemed to come to a complete halt. Her calls to her grandmother went unanswered and eventually went straight to voicemail; in the end, they remained unreturned, and all was quiet on their end. Going back to school the first full week of January, her lower lids carried deep circles caused by the numerous sleepless nights, and she considered if it might be time to restock her makeup supply in an attempt to hide her condition.

Her peers seemed oblivious to the events, only taking note of them as an oddity. A few found mentioning the ice storm would distract teachers away from their intended lessons, under the guise of *current-event* discussions, and these became frequent, leaving the girl feeling forlorn. Several of the staff were as delusional as the members of The Ranch and had no qualms informing their students that mankind was doomed to perish, either by fire or by ice.

Deciding the girl needed a distraction, Caleb packed her pistol, along with the one that he had purchased for himself, into one of the saddlebags on his bike for a Saturday outing. Carrying a few boxes of shells, he announced, "It's time!"

"Time for what?" she answered in the typical, dejected tone she used as of late.

"I'm taking you to the gun range. It's time you learned to use your gift." He smiled, hoping to draw her in.

Glaring at him with hollow eyes, she briefly wondered if she should be afraid something was wrong but then recalled he had given her the weapon before the country had started to descend into chaos. "All right. I guess I can do that." Donning her coat, she pulled on her gloves and mentally prepared herself for the ride to the range.

Arriving at the open-air facility outside of town, Caleb used his code to enter the gate. Pulling up next to the row of covered tables, he slid off the bike and turned slowly, looking the place over and finding it deserted. "I guess no one likes t' shoot in the cold. I figured there'd be other people here."

"Bunch of pansies around here." She flickered a tiny grin. "They don't like to do anything in the cold, and it's not even freezing yet."

"Yeah, I get that," he agreed. "Ok, little bit. Le's see what you can do with this thing."

Filling the clip, he inserted it into the gun. Directing her where to stand, his hand wafted at the metal bars that held a variety of metal targets, all in the shapes of miniature animals and set at various distances. "Hold it in your hands, like we practiced. Then give the trigger a slow, steady squeeze until it fires. An' most importantly, never point a gun at someone you don' intend t' shoot." He wafted a hand at the targets. "An' o' course, when you do…shoot t' kill."

"Yes, I remember." She thought about the lessons he had given her at the house before they made the ride out. Holding up the pistol, she stared down the sights and slowly squeezed, her heart leaping out of control when the bang occurred, with her hands jerking wildly at the same time.

"Nice," he praised her. "You still hit the little target, but you need to work on holdin' the gun still. You know it's gonna recoil, so put the effort into keepin' it steady in case you have t' shoot more than once."

Taking his advice to heart, she continued to pling the tiny targets closest to her. When they were all gone, she moved to the next row, even filling the clip for herself when it had been emptied. "Am I doing any better?"

"You're doin' fine." He had moved behind her to get a better feel for her point of view, and his hands lightly rested on her hips in front of him.

Firing three more shots, they did not land anywhere near her targets, and she whined slightly, "Caleb…you're distracting me."

"Whaddaya mean, distracting you?"

"I mean exactly that." She shifted so that his hands slid around to her back and belly. "I'm not used to people touching me." She grimaced. "It's throwing off my shot."

"Oh." He grinned widely. "I'll step away then," and he put a few feet between them. "Is this far enough?"

Shaking her head, she returned to her practice, going for targets further away. Continuing, she could only hit about half at the twenty-foot range, and Caleb waved her off. "I think tha's good enough, little bit. You got a feel for it, an' we need t' save up more ammo before we spend any more of it on practice."

"Is it really that hard to get?"

"Yeah." His brow furrowed. "I think there's quite a few of us here locally tryin' t' stock up, so every delivery that comes in gets bought out as soon as it arrives."

"Wow." She handed him the pistol. "Are you going to show me how to clean it?"

He grinned at her approvingly. "Sure. Soon as we get home, I'll take you through th' process."

Putting their gear away and climbing back on his bike, the couple made the trek home, Bailey feeling an odd sense of pride at her accomplishment that day. *I don't know what my parents were so afraid of. Shooting is actually pretty easy, and someday knowing how might come in handy.* Holding him snugly while they rode, her thoughts churned, wondering what else her best friend had to teach her.

Things rocked on, and by the end of the next week, it finally began to feel like winter in west Texas. Bailey walked beside Caleb, headed towards their apartment a few minutes after midnight. He had been hanging out at the shop as usual, ready to share the short jaunt home with her at the end of her shift. At the light, he unexpectedly reached to take her hand. "Hey, little bit." His breath frosted, and he gave her digits a squeeze through her glove. "Are you doin' ok?"

"Of course. Why wouldn't I be?" She allowed him to hold her, guiding her across the patches of ice that had formed on the sidewalk, despite the preventative sand scattered across it.

"I dunno," he jokingly replied. "Maybe that huge ice storm that's been hangin' around." He grinned at her, noting the lines crinkling her features. "I'm worried about you. You seem t' be taking all o' this really hard. The country's faced worse." He released her hand, moving it to her back while she gripped the rail and climbed the stairs.

"I know," she sighed the words, "but things are different now. Did you know we are no longer serving chicken strips at the store? Guess why."

"I don't have a clue." He chuckled. "So, tell me why."

"Because all the ice up north has disrupted the freight lines, so there weren't any on the last two trucks," she replied crisply, removing her jacket and other gear, hanging them on the hooks. "I'm off tomorrow night by the way. Are you working tomorrow?"

"No." He hung his own jacket. "It's too cold for pourin' concrete, so it may be a week or two before I'm doin' anything but hangin' out." His eyes darted around the small living room. "We should do some serious shopping in the morning. I mean, stock the cabinets an' freezer as full as we can."

"Why would we do that?" Her eyes grew wide, certain she knew the answer.

"It's only a precaution." He smiled. "Better t' be safe, right?"

"If we really wanted to be safe, we would get the hell out of here."

"Whadda you mean?" he demanded, feeling as if she had knocked the wind out of him.

"My grandparents don't answer the phone, Caleb. They haven't since before the storm moved in. We're getting fewer and fewer things at the store because our supply lines are compromised. That little ice storm has lasted three solid weeks, and there's no end in sight." She inhaled deeply, having thought about this for days. "I'm not saying they're right. But maybe we should pack up and head south."

The man glared at her for several seconds, allowing her words to sink in. "I think you're overreacting. We'll go in the morning an' stock up on necessities. If things aren't looking up by the first o' February..." He paused, not sure he wanted to commit to a date. "Yeah, we'll talk about it if things don' seem better by then. Besides, if you leave, you don' get your credit for th' year. An' that's the whole reason we're here, remember?"

Puckering her lips, the girl knew he was right. However, getting credit seemed pretty low on her list of priorities when their lives were at stake. "Fine. We'll do some shopping after my training." Leaving him where he stood, she made her way down the hall, closing her door a little more loudly than necessary behind her.

Stretching out on her bed, she stared at her trembling digits, flexing them into fists slowly. *What the hell is wrong with me?* she reflected to herself. *He's right. Maybe I am making too much out of this.* Closing her eyes, she breathed deeply, focused on relaxing and trying to get some much-needed sleep.

The following morning, the pair hit the gym, then had their breakfast. As soon as the dishes were loaded, they climbed onto his bike and made for the H-E-B located a few blocks down from their apartment. The parking lot teamed with traffic as usual, and he slid the bike into one of the narrow spaces labeled *compact car.*

"Watch the ice." He grabbed her arm, noting the gloss on the black surface.

"I see it." She gripped him, leaning towards him as they scooted their way inside. "I guess winter has finally come to Texas."

Moving through the sliding glass, he caught the end of a shopping cart, pulling it along behind them. "We may have t' make two trips."

"Naw, I got my bus pass," she answered calmly. "We can load it all on there, and I'll meet you at the house." She wore a small smile, glad that they were at least doing something productive.

A few aisles later, her grimace had returned. Fighting their way between the laden carts, the noise level in the store seemed exaggerated, and she mumbled, "Seems like we're not the only ones wanting to get stocked up."

"Yeah." Caleb bobbed his golden spikes in agreement. "We're not the only ones." He scowled, wondering if she had been right about getting out of town. The shelves appeared light, with quite a few products completely wiped. "If you're takin' the bus, le's get some boxed goods. You know, pasta an' stuff. It keeps for months, an' we got tons o' cabinet space open."

Cutting her eyes over at him, the suggestion did not make her feel any more comfortable. "What about canned goods?"

"Sure. We can do that, too," he agreed.

Loading up the basket as high as they could, they finally made their way to the front, where the lines were four and five carts deep, end to end. "Wow, these guys are really raking it in," she observed.

"Yeah," Caleb exhaled his agreement, his eyes darting warily about them. "Reminds me of the day before Thanksgiving, t' be honest."

Almost an hour later, they wheeled the cart filled with plastic bags out the front of the store. "Where does the bus stop, I wonder." He shaded his eyes as he swung his gaze around, noting the drizzle that had started to fall, coating everything with a thin sheet of ice while they were inside.

"Over there, across the street." She pointed, trying to ease the cart that way.

Using half of the bar, he helped her, getting across in the traffic turning out to be the biggest challenge. Taking their time, they pushed the cart to the light and doubled back on the other side to be safe. When they finally arrived at the glass cubicle, he slid his arms around her, aware of her shivers. Holding her tightly against his larger frame with his back to the opening to block the wind further, he frowned. "How long?"

"One an hour." She indicated the sign. "We're in luck, and it should be here any minute. Any slower, and we'd be waiting another hour."

"Man, this sucks. Pete shoulda gotten you a car," he complained in a low tone.

"I think he was afraid of the traffic," she made the excuse, not caring to voice the real reason she figured the choice had been made.

"Anyways," he growled and indicated the large transport ambling towards them, "le's get all this on board, an' I'll meet you at the bus stop to unload it. How long between here an' there, do you think?"

"About twenty minutes, in good weather," she agreed, sliding into the seat after they were loaded. "I'll see you there."

SEVENTEEN

Close to Home

HAVING THEIR KITCHEN FULLY STOCKED, the couple relaxed into the evening, as the girl seemed to have calmed down a bit after their morning adventure. "Le's watch a movie tonight," Caleb offered. "You know, take our minds off o' the real stuff for a while."

"Sure," she reluctantly agreed. "But I want to check on the boys first." Making her way into their room, she pulled up the connection and flipped through her uncle's latest posts. She noted that the weather seemed to be above freezing in the little community, and she recalled that Caleb had told her he had only seen snow there twice in his lifetime.

Noting that the tall blond leaned on the door frame, observing her, she smiled. "They're pretty safe there, aren't they?"

"Well, that's why that location was chosen. Pretty isolated, which means most o' what threatens other places can't quite reach them." He moved in closer, perching on the bunk next to her. "That's a nice lookin' little pony," he observed the boys grooming their little Star.

Flipping over to his page, Bailey noted that Amanda had tagged him in another pic of her huge belly, captioned *Any Day Now*.

"She shouldn'a done that. She's practically makin' my case for me."

"What's that supposed to mean?" The girl next to him clicked her own profile to remove the eyesore and opened her mailbox. Noting that her grandmother never had responded to her message, months old now, she emitted a small sigh.

"It means if she's havin' that kid any day now, there's no way it could be mine, even if I had slept with her. Nine months ago, I was here spyin' on you."

Her jaw dropped slightly, her auburn hair shimmered when she raised her chin to stare at him. She asked in a hushed tone, "So, no one else has noticed the discrepancy?"

"I'm tellin' you, it's a game. Somehow, they're manipulatin' this. Either that or she really thinks they'll believe her over me. O' course, if that was her plan, she should be claimin' the baby's not due for at least another month. That'd mean it coulda been mine, since we were back at The Ranch in June."

"I don't know, Caleb." She shook her locks again. "It all sounds fishy to me. But for the record, I believe you." She reached over, laying her hand lightly over his.

"Since when?" he replied in surprise, her gesture putting him on edge.

"Since"—she paused, removing her appendage and placing it on the mouse—"I discovered this." She flipped to the picture she had come across that one of the other girls had posted. It was an older one, lost in the files from days gone by, showing Amanda and Luis in quite the comfy position. She faced the man, her arms around his neck, while Don had an arm around her, sandwiching the girl between them. "Quite the little trollop, isn't she?" she said quietly to herself.

"Yeah. Only I didn't know. Not for a long time." He stared at the screen, not aware that the picture had ever existed. "I guess I was the last one t' find out." Cutting his eyes over at her clear, green orbs, he smiled. "It's ok, though. I figured it out, an' her little game ain't gonna get her anywhere. Now, how about that movie?"

In silent agreement, Bailey closed out the page and shut down the machine. "Find us something fun, maybe on the pay per view, and I'll make us dinner."

Sitting down to small steaks at the table a short time later, he grinned. "Have I tol' you what a good cook you are?"

"Yes," she replied. "Quite a few times, actually," but she smiled that it pleased him. "What movie did we get?"

"The Lone Ranger." His eyes danced. "I heard it wasn't very good, but I wanna give it a try."

"You nut." She chuckled, happy in the moment she could share with him, allowing it to lift her spirits after the disheartening post on his page.

A couple of hours later, the show came to an end, and they both laughed at the crazy flick. "Well, I won't say it was good, but it wasn't bad, either," he chortled.

Bailey agreed, turning the channel over to catch the local news at ten. A few minutes later, they both sat, eyes glued to the screen in horror. *"Authorities say that the outbreak has been contained, but so far, over one hundred cases have been confirmed. Whether or not classes will resume on Monday remains to be seen."*

"Holy shit," Caleb breathed, realizing the anchor was talking about one of the junior high schools in Odessa. "That's pretty fucking close to home!"

"Yes, it is," the girl agreed, suddenly too restless to sit still and snapping the bad news box off in disgust. "Caleb, I don't like this. I don't want to wait until February. I want you to take me to The Ranch *now.*"

Air caught in his lungs as he stared at her. "Ok." Then he inhaled deeply, forcing the organs to work. "But it may be a few days before I can arrange it. I don' wanna just show up with you. Not until we have some word that they're not gonna do anything to you."

"Fine," she tossed crisply. "But we can't stay here. I don't want to be in the middle of all of this…" She wafted her hand around, indicating the crowded metropolis that lay beyond the walls of their domicile. "I'm not going to school Monday, either."

"Now, wait." He held up a hand. "They said everything had been contained, an' there's no reason to quit livin' our lives an' bein' normal—"

"No way," she cut him off. "Sure it's contained, until it happens again. People are dying from that shit, and we are packed in here like sardines. Even going to the store, like we did today, could put us at risk. Not to mention going to sit in a bunch of classrooms with thirty or forty students in each one with me."

"They have that many in your classes?" he asked in surprise.

"Don't change the subject!" she exclaimed. "And yeah, every class has at least thirty kids in it, and we sit a foot or less apart, so if one of them brings it in, we're all in a world of hurt. I can't stand the thought of it." She shuddered violently while resisting the urge to wash her hands at that exact moment.

"Wow," he breathed, reaching over to massage her knee. "I'm so sorry. I knew you were havin' issues." He gave her a squeeze. "But I didn' realize it was this bad." He stared at her, removing his hand. "I'll call an' talk t' my dad, an' your uncle if I need to. See what they say about it. If they won' let us go down there, maybe we could hold up here for a week or two an' see what comes of it."

"Oh my God." She clutched her hair, pulling it away from her face. "I can't imagine being trapped in here for weeks with nothing to do." Glancing over at the blackened screen, her brow furrowed. "Watching a never-ending deluge of doom and gloom isn't any more appealing, either."

"Ok, little bit." He pulled out his phone, half hoping he would get their voicemail. "Go get a shower an' try t' calm down," he instructed her, knowing listening to his end of the conversation wouldn't help her in that department.

Reluctantly, Bailey moved to comply, leaving the man on the couch. Inside the bathroom, she stripped down, her hands trembling when she reached for the knob. *Damn. At least at The Ranch we would have a purpose. Chores we can do instead of go stir crazy.* She thought of the animals in the barn and horses that would need tending. *Yes, I would much rather be there.*

Out on the sofa, Caleb put the phone up to his ear. Peter Mason answered the line on the second ring, "Hello?" his voice sounding anxious.

"Hey, Pete. How are things down south?"

"Caleb? Do you have any idea what time it is? Why the hell are you callin' me t' ask such an asinine question as that?"

"Well"—the younger man exhaled lightly, listening to the sound of water spraying in the other room—"because it's lookin' like all hell's gonna break loose here any day now, an' I was hopin' me an' Bailey could come home."

"Naw, I can't condone that. Not right now," the girl's uncle answered quietly. "I can bring it up to a few people, get a feel o' where everyone stands now that they've had time to get used to the idea of her joining us. An' she's been a good girl." He exhaled in an exaggerated manner. "Let me call you back in a day or two. I can let you know more then."

Caleb sat staring off into space when Bailey rejoined him.

"So, what did they say?" She sank down on to the cushion, a towel in hand to catch the drips from her hair.

"They said they'll get back to us. In a day or two," he stipulated. "They wanna be sure you'll be accepted before they give their word."

Nodding, she agreed quietly. "Ok. I'll try to hang on here the best I can. I'll go to work and to school until we find out more. That is if we don't get a snow day."

"A snow day?"

"Sure. A bunch of the kids have been talking about it nonstop since the weather turned bad up north. Apparently, a little bit of ice on the ground and everything around here shuts down," she explained. "Back home, we go anyways." She chuckled. "Of course, what's happening in Lincoln right now is a lot worse than anything I've ever seen." She pictured the latest newscast in disgust.

"Yup," he agreed. "I heard some are really callin' this a hundred-year storm, only supposed t' happen once a century—three weeks o' solid deep freeze across seven states an' no sign o' lettin' up. Don' worry, little bit. We'll get it worked out."

"I know." She smiled softly, grateful for his caring. "I'm really glad that you're here with me. I can't imagine having to face all of this alone."

"You'd be all right." He stood, heading towards the hall, only pausing to check the door on his way by. "You're a smart girl. An' you're strong. I know you like havin' me t' look out for you, but you could do it on your own if you had to."

"Probably," she agreed, standing to join him, "but that doesn't mean that I would like it."

EIGHTEEN

Rock the Boat

THE FOLLOWING DAY, Peter made his way down to see John, not even waiting until breakfast had been served. "Missed you at the gym this mornin'," he called to the other man, glaring at Martha across her kitchen for a moment before she picked up on the vibe and steered Carson and herself out of the room. "Somethin's goin' on." He took a chair and spoke in a lower tone after the pair left. "Caleb called me at damn near midnight last night. Says that all hell's about to break loose. You know anything about it?"

"Only what I see on th' news," his comrade grunted. "Sure was disappointed in that boy."

"Well, don't be," Pete admonished. "That 'Manda's a liar an' always has been. I's glad when they broke up, an' I got no problem believing that he ain't the father of that baby. The problem is who it could be. Havin' Bailey come in here wasn't the worse that coulda happened to us, an' you damn well know it."

"What's that suposta mean?" John squinted at him for a long moment. "You know somethin' you ain' tellin' me?"

"Only that claiming it was his'd be the easy way out. We got a lot o' families packed in here. If it turned out to be one of the *menfolk's* doin's, that'd put a real crimp in everyone's attitudes."

"Yeah, or if it turned out t' be yurs," the other man charged. "She says it's Caleb's, an' until I get proof otherwise, that's how it is. Anything else you'd like t' discuss?"

Pete frowned. "You know, we've been working on this a lot of years, you an' me. We put every dime we made into building this place—building a refuge for our families when they need it." He pointed a stiff digit at his best friend. "You think about that, an' then you give your son a call. Tell him t' bring Bailey an' get down here where it's safe while they still can."

Standing, he gave his sandy curls a shake in disgust, heading out the door and onto the porch. "Martha, you have time for a word?" He patted Carson on the head.

"I suppose I do." She glanced back at the screen, then stepped off the porch, walking towards the greenhouse, Peter catching up and walking stiffly beside her. "What's it you wanna discuss?" she asked when they were inside the large structure.

"I think you know that baby don't belong t' Caleb," he got right to the point.

The woman shrugged, turning towards a row of potted plants. Pushing her thumb into the dirt to see if they needed water, she responded calmly, "I can't help you with that, Pete. Things are goin' perdy smooth right now. Why you gotta rock th' boat?"

"Because my niece's life's at stake," he shot back evenly. "An' maybe your son's. Just…talk to John about it. Tell him what you think, an' see if you guys can figure something out. Before it's too late." Leaving her to her chores, he stomped down the road, completing the short distance to his own house and his meal with the boys he had come to think of as his own.

Bailey rolled out of bed, feeling groggy. Putting on her clothes for the gym, she opened her door and listened. Hearing the sound of the man in the other room, she drew a deep breath, trying to calm her nerves.

As soon as he was out, she planted herself next to him while he moved around, setting up the coffee pot for when they returned.

Staring at his hands, she confessed, "I had a dream last night."

"A dream, huh?" He chuckled. "You're not one o' those people who thinks they actually mean somethin', are you?"

Looking up at his clear blue eyes, she gripped the edge of the cabinet next to her. "No, not normally. But with the way things have been going, I thought I should bring it up."

"You know"—he stopped in mid movement, dropping the pack of filters onto the countertop—"I really care about you, Bailey. So I don' want you to take this the wrong way. But you're actin' like a big baby over all o' this end o' the world shit. Do you really think that's what's hapnin' here? 'Cause I don't." He slapped the laminate, causing her to jump. Lifting the white package, he returned his fingers to fumbling in an effort to remove one.

Her jaw dropped, she glared at him, confused by his profession of caring followed by his harsh reprimand. "So what would you like for me to do about it?" she stammered. "You don't even want to hear what I dreamed?"

"No, I don't," he quibbled, finishing with the machine and indicating the door. "Le's get over to the gym. You can take your anger out on me while we train."

Taking him up on his offer, she pushed herself beyond belief, doing everything she could to lay into him. By the time they had finished, her arms and legs were exhausted. *And this is only the training. The workout comes later.*

Sprawling out on the mat next to her, Caleb stared at the ceiling. "You're really tough when you're pissed. You still wanna tell me 'bout your dream?"

"Not really." She pouted slightly. "It doesn't matter. You make it sound like everything happening around us is normal or that I shouldn't be worried about it."

"Well, I don't think it's normal," he replied, getting to his feet and offering her his hand. "But worryin' about it ain' gonna help." Hauling her up next to him, he paused, staring into her clear green orbs. "I'm really scared, little bit," he admitted in a quiet whisper.

Meeting his gaze, she inhaled sharply. "Why? You really think this could be it?"

"I don't know," he confessed with a shrug, grabbing her jacket and handing it to her, along with her pants. "I mean, most scenarios have some catastrophic event, somethin' that happens, an' the world spins into chaos in a day or two. Like this, it's like watchin' it happen in slow motion. You know what happens to a frog when you put him in a pot o' boilin' water?"

Reaching for the door, the girl shook her long waves. "Sorry, I can't say that I do. Other than it would probably kill it."

"Well, if the pot's boilin', the frog jumps out, so no, it don't kill it. It knows as soon as it hits that he don' belong there." He reached over, looping his fingers with hers. "But you put that same frog in a pot o' cool water an' bring it to a boil, he dies."

Bailey frowned, releasing his digits at the door of their home. "So, what are you getting at?" afraid of what his analogy referred to.

"Well, we're the frog. Mankind that is. If we were dumped into a pot o' boilin' water, we'd know that it was gonna kill us, an' we would jump, no question about it." He moved towards the kitchen, taking a cup of the brew he had set up before they left. "But that's not what's goin' on around us. Things are hapnin', but it's not all at once. Like raising the temperature nice an' slow. We won't notice the boil cause it don' feel that different than it did yesterday."

"So you're saying all of these things are only the beginning, and the water's just starting to get warm?" She stared at him, amazed by the simplicity of the comparison.

"Maybe." He took a noisy sip. "While you were asleep, havin' your dream, I was awake last night. My mind was too full o' things, past an' present, an' I jus' let it go. An' that's what I came up with. We're jus' like that damned frog."

"Ok, so we know that the water's warming. What do we do about it?"

"This isn't the warming, little bit. This's the boil. The waters been warming for years now, an' man's been too comfortable in it to notice. Little signs, small changes, an' we've been ignoring them. Or adjusting to them, like creating FEMA. Reacting, rather than fixing the problem." He inhaled deeply, exhaling noisily through his nose. "You're right. We can't stay here. But I'm not sure we can go to The Ranch, either. Within three days, we're leaving…either way."

"So where're we gonna go if we can't go there?" she demanded loudly, suddenly in full on panic. "We don't even have a car! All we have is your bike, which offers us no protection from the elements."

"I know." He nodded slightly. "That's what I've been tryin' t' figure out. So please don' think that I'm not takin' this seriously. We need a plan before we act, tha's all."

Staring up at his clear blue eyes, his words suddenly made sense. Throwing her arms around his neck, she pulled him against her, stroking his short golden stubble that ran along the nape of his neck. "You think my brothers are going to be ok?" she breathed against his shoulder.

"Yeah, little bit. They're gonna be fine." He pulled her firmly against him. "We're the ones that're gonna need savin'."

NINETEEN

Love Thy Neighbor

BAILEY WENT in to work that evening, unsure what else to do. She had come to care for her place of employment very deeply over the last few months, and some of her co-workers were people she thought of as friends. Slowly putting her bag in her locker and moving to the floor to take her post at the register, she wondered if she should mention to them what Caleb had said and that they were in danger.

Arriving at her spot, she swiped her card, and Mark immediately presented himself next to her. Pointing at a list taped to the side of her machine, he indicated the menu behind them. "We've marked most everything that we're out of..." he began.

Her mouth hung open as she stared at the sign. "We can make burgers, but we're out of tomatoes and pickles, and plain French fries only. That's it?"

"Yeah." He chuckled lightly, turning his palms to the ceiling. "I called the main office when the truck got here with almost nothing on it, but they said it's out of their hands. We got what there is to be had. So"—he nodded at his favorite employee—"give them your best smile and do what you can."

He turned to walk away, but she called softly, "Wait!"

"What?" he stopped, slightly irritated that she needed further instruction.

"We should leave," she replied lamely. Stepping closer to him, she lowered her voice, "It's not safe here. There's too many people and not enough supplies. It's going to get dangerous."

He blinked at her, stunned by what she suggested. "So you're saying we should all just…leave town?"

"Yes." She cast her bright green eyes around at the others, a few of whom were staring at her. "We need to go, now, while we still can."

Frowning, he shook his head. "Maybe you need another night off." He reached for her card to swipe it for her and close her out of the drawer.

"You don't believe me?" she stammered.

"No, Bailey," his tone remained cross, his voice raised. "You're not making any sense. Where would we go, do you think? There's a couple o' hundred thousand people here in Midland, alone. And Odessa and Andrews and Big Springs. There's what, nearly a million people in a fifty-mile radius? Where're we all gonna go?" Wafting his hand at her, he ratcheted his voice down, noticing the stares. "Just get out. Go home and rest. Come back tomorrow…or don't." Turning his back on her, he went to make a few phone calls to try and replace her shift.

Retrieving her purse, she hesitated for a moment, a sick feeling in her gut, as if she had suddenly lost something dear to her—forever. Walking briskly back to the apartment, she stumbled inside to find Caleb sitting in the man chair, chest bare and flipping through the channels. Gaping at her after she entered, he stammered, "What're you doing back so early?"

"They're out of food. They are serving meat, bread, and French fries. I left," she put it succinctly, not bothering to explain her momentary meltdown. "I'm not going back. I tried to warn Mark that it was a bad sign, and he just stared at me, telling me I was crazy."

"He didn' believe you," her roommate sympathized.

"No." She shook her head. "It's not that he doesn't believe. He's hopeless, I think. He doesn't see any way out, so he isn't even going to try. He's going to stay there, selling burgers, until the entire place is bare."

"Wow." Caleb ran his hand through his short spikes, then down across his smooth chest. "I've heard o' that—people in th' middle of a catastrophe not leavin' their post 'cause they can't fathom what's goin' on around them."

"It's crazy," she replied. "So, I'm not going to school tomorrow. I'm going to go clean out my bank account, instead. We can take the cash and buy a vehicle of some kind. Something that can provide some protection when we head south."

"That sounds an awful lot like what I was sittin' here thinkin'." He nodded, his head bobbing in an odd circle. "We can pack up what we have here in the house, foodwise, an' take it with us. Plus, we need water an' lots of it."

"Agreed." She moved to the kitchen, preparing to cook some of the frozen items for their dinner. "People can live for weeks with no food but only three days without water, max."

"You've been reading up on th' subject, have you?"

"No," she replied, adjusting the oven. "I've been paying attention."

He smiled. "Ok, I've got about fifteen thousand in my account. We may be able t' get a really decent vehicle for that. We don' want anything that'd break down on us."

"We should finance it," she replied, putting vegetable medley into a pan to boil.

"Finance," he grimaced. "Why? What if they won' let us?"

"If they won't, we can use the cash." She flicked her eyes over at his hand resting on his heaving chest, finally ready to mention it. "Could you go put a shirt on please?"

"A shirt on? What the hell for? I thought we were talkin' about gettin' a vehicle."

"We are," she agreed, "but where I grew up, walking around without a shirt on wasn't condoned. Please." She cut her eyes over at him. "Go put one on."

"I've been walkin' around here without one every day for months, and now it bothers you?" He grinned from ear to ear. "Or you want me to leave the room for some reason?" he eyed her suspiciously. "Anyway, please," he cajoled her advice. "Why should we finance the car?"

"Because"—she rolled her eyes at his refusal to get dressed—"if they finance it, we still have the cash, and if they don't, we pay cash for it. Either way, we get the car, but with the loan, we have the ability to buy more supplies to take with us."

"Tha's a good plan," he agreed with an exaggerated nod. "I'll be right back," he called through the window to her as he sauntered down the hall. Locating a clean button-down in the closet, he returned to the kitchen a few minutes later, adjusting the collar and fastening the front.

Sliding into a chair to watch her, he smirked. "So, why didn' you say somethin' before? If it bothered you t' see me half naked."

"It doesn't bother me," she lied flatly. "I didn't want to come across that I wanted to boss you around." Glancing over at him, she smiled. "But thank you for getting dressed."

"Was that an 'up north' thing or your parents' idea?"

"I think it was a class thing," her reply almost sounded cheeky. "I mean social class, not...class, class. My parents wanted us to be a part of the upper crust, or at least my mother did. I'm not sure what my father wanted, beyond always working to please her."

"Oh," he clipped the word and dropped his chin for a moment.

"Well, in that case, I should tell you there won' be any classes in a few months. There won' be much of anything, for that matter."

"I know," she agreed readily, then cut her eyes over to take him in. "And I have to admit I've been a lot happier since I stopped trying to be what my mom always wanted me to be."

"Oh yeah?"

"Yes." She grinned. "I haven't had makeup on my face since the first morning I spent at The Ranch, and I don't really miss it."

"I don't miss it either." He showed her his teeth as well. "You look real pretty without it, Bailey-girl."

Placing their dinner on the table, she reached for the plates. "Well, I'm glad. So, once we get a vehicle and pack it full of supplies, we can head south? Or do you have somewhere else in mind?"

"South," he agreed, serving himself. "I want to get there before anything ultra-crazy happens."

"Are you going to tell them that we're coming?"

"No." He squinted at her for a moment. "I don' think it'll matter either way. Besides, I've called twice today, an' neither my father nor your uncle answer the phone."

"Well, that's no surprise," she said between bites. "Neither of my phones got service out there."

"Neither? You had more than one?"

"Yes," she admitted quietly. "It's a long story, and the point is, I don't think them not answering means anything. I think it's the location."

Caleb shook his head, wondering if he should mention what he knew. Finally, making his choice, he admitted quietly, "Pete shut your phone off. That's why you didn't get any service. They were afraid of who you might contact…and why."

"You're kidding me." She stared at him, fork suspended for a moment in mid-air, anger washing over her before she pushed it aside. "Well, what about the other one? I had gotten a pay-as-you-go phone, and it didn't have service either."

"Well, did you pay th' bill?"

"Yes, as far as I know. Maybe that means the one I have now isn't going to work either. Maybe The Ranch is outside their area." She pondered the idea, unhappy that she would lose contact with the outside world again.

"Yeah, well, who're you gonna call, anyways?" He laughed at the idea. "Shit!" He slammed his fist on the table. "I forgot about your grandparents!"

"Oh my God," she breathed. "I did, too. And they haven't answered the phone since I talked to Nanna before the ice storm hit."

Caleb placed his elbows on the table, leaning his chin against his hands. "I don't know what to do about them, little bit. I don't know that there's anything we can do."

Realizing he was right, her eyes grew misty, and a tear slid down her cheek. "It's ok." She sniffed. "I know it would be stupid to head north, even if we thought we could get to them."

"Yeah," he agreed in a soft tone. "We'll be doin' good if we can save ourselves. There's a lot o' road between us an' The Ranch—a large number o' things that could happen t' prevent us from gettin' there."

Her eyes wide, she stared across the table at him, her appetite gone. "I shouldn't have said anything at the store tonight. What if someone there comes after us or wants us to take them with us?"

"We won't." He shook his head, fingers pressed against his lips. "We can't save everyone, an' it would only make our situation worse if we tried. Don't tell anyone else what we're planning. We get the car tomorrow an' leave tomorrow night. Travel after dark an' try to push through."

"Ok," she agreed, standing to clear the table.

"You're not gonna eat that?" He indicated her unfinished meal.

"I'm not hungry," she admitted quietly, the thought of what lay ahead of them stealing her appetite away.

"You should eat it anyways." He stared up at her. "We may have some lean times ahead of us."

Glaring down at the plate, she hoped he wasn't right but feared that he was. Sitting down, she managed to eat a bit more, while the conversation had come to an abrupt end.

TWENTY

Way Down South

CALEB WOKE Bailey before her alarm went off, his nerves not allowing him to wait any longer. Joining him in the living room a few minutes later, she donned her jeans and a long-sleeved tee. "You want breakfast now or when we get back?"

"Now," he agreed, checking the time. "It's almost five. That gives us an hour to eat an' get over t' Wal-Mart. We can get some storage bins to put all this food in that we're taking with us. The buses start to run at six, an' we can get them back here the same way we did the other day."

"Ok," she agreed, setting out the skillet. Opening the fridge, she pulled out eggs and sausage. "We won't be able to take the perishables with us, will we?"

"Probably not." He shook his head. "Better if we avoid anything that might spoil, unless we end up with tons o' room left over. Since we still don't know what vehicle we're gonna get, we might as well eat this an' save th' canned an' dry goods t' take with us."

Whipping up the meal, the girl did her best to remain calm, continuing with the small talk. "Did you think of anything else we need to do while we're there?"

"Well, we're gonna need some water bottles. We can get some now, empty so they're easier t' carry, an' fill 'em after we get the car. They got those water things all over town."

"Ok." She nodded, stirring the eggs. "I like that idea. So we need a roll of quarters. Hey, maybe the store won't be so crowded this early in the day, either."

"I'm sure it won' be," he agreed with her assessment, "but we wanna get everything we can now 'cause it will be later, an' we don' wanna fight with that if we can avoid it." He wrung his hands periodically, helping her by making and buttering the toast to keep them busy.

Finally seated, the pair ate hungrily, her appetite returned after her light dinner. Scraping off the plates, she rinsed them and loaded the dishwasher out of habit, giving it a start. "I guess that wasn't necessary." She grimaced. "We won't be back here again after today."

"You never know," he praised. "An' it didn' hurt. Grab your jacket, an' le's get rollin'."

A few minutes later, they pulled into the Wal-mart parking lot. Caleb could feel his pulse in his neck when he surveyed the number of cars on the far end, gathered around the door. Finding a space, it would be a small hike to the entrance, an oddity at the ungodly hour of five in the morning.

"Are these all employees?" Bailey asked in a mystified tone.

"The other doors are locked until seven," he informed her as they made their way towards the front. "Tha's why it looks like so many cars. Everyone is bunched together on this end."

"Oh," she accepted his reasoning. "Well, at least they're open twenty-four hours." She grinned. Inside, she stopped, staring at the store in dismay. "Wow, this place is a mess!" Glaring at the aisles, she couldn't believe her eyes. Or the number of patrons milling about. "Uh, Caleb. This is actually…a lot of people."

Standing in awe for a moment, he reached to clasp her fingers. "It's ok. Get a basket, an' we'll get what we need an' go."

Pushing the cart, the couple took the path that passed along the front, headed for the housewares side of the massive shopping center. Locating the aisle that held the water bottles, they discovered only three remained on the shelf, and he quickly snatched them. "Wow, this place is picked over already!"

"Yeah." A man in a blue vest passing by laughed at him. "Everyone's gettin' stocked for the storm!"

"What storm?" Caleb gaped at him, unsure what he was referring to. *Maybe we quit watching the news too soon.*

"That big cold front, goofy." The guy's eyes darted, taking the younger man in from head to toe in disbelief. "By six o'clock tonight, ninety-percent o' the South's supposta be sittin' under a couple o' foot o' snow."

"The South, huh?" he gave a brief retort, reaching for their basket with a fresh sense of urgency.

"Yup." He grinned lopsidedly. "From Florida all the way t' us. I don' believe it myself, but apparently somebody does." His open palm indicated what remained of their inventory. "Jus' wait 'til you get to the food aisles." He tossed a thumb over his shoulder in that direction. "It's a circus over there. Thank God I work in hardware!" Something about the man's laugh made Caleb's flesh crawl.

His jaw set, his eyes shifted over at his companion, and he moved closer to growl, "I think we need t' get our stuff an' get movin'."

Bailey nodded, claiming an empty cart that had been abandoned close by and following him to the rear of the store. Finding the plastic containers, they located a few of the ones they wanted and the covers that fit them. Hustling to the other side, where the food items were located, it looked as if a bomb had gone off, and navigating became much more difficult.

"I can't believe all these people!" she hissed, leaning closer to her comrade. "It's so early!"

"I think they must be really scared. As soon as we get back to the apartment, we need t' get a line on this new storm situation!"

Pushing their carts, they managed to work their way down a few of the rows. Choosing a large multipack of individual water bottles, Caleb tossed that on the rack under his cart.

Weaving their way, they picked up another box of trash bags for packing the rest of the household items. Deciding to take more canned goods while they were there, they discovered a group of people raking everything that they saw into one of their baskets.

Fighting to get ahead of them, Caleb began to do the same, grabbing any and every can he could get his hands on. "Hey, little bit. Get over on the next aisle an' get as many o' those meat stuffs as you can!"

Pushing her cart, she fought her way around the corner, earning a scowl from a very large woman who pushed a basket full of dry goods after she had bumped into her. "Sorry," the girl remembered her manners, and adjusted her basket to allow the lady to pass. Standing at the end of the shelving, she glared in disbelief, then swung the basket over to the next, grabbing boxed dinners instead.

When she found her way back to him, Caleb glared at her heaping pile. "Where's all the meat?"

"Gone." She breathed a disgusted noise out her nose. "Someone got there first! Do you really think they'll have snow in Florida?" she tossed out, her mind running in circles while she plucked a hand-crank can opener from a hook.

"With th' crazy weather we've been seein', I wouldn' say no," he scowled, grabbing a second. Pausing, he noted that she looked panicked and wished he could take back his part in it. "Honestly, I wish I hadn't said that I'd like t' see an Ice Age. I really didn' mean it that way…" His voice trailed away with the confession.

"I know you didn't." She stepped closer and ran her hand across his back, with a makeshift squeeze for an embrace.

Catching her appendage, he drew her in and held her firmly, feeling a tingle of connection between them. "We're gonna make it, little bit." His blue orbs dropped to her lips, and his fingers sifted through a handful of auburn curls, pulling her into a private world where the chaos that swarmed around them didn't exist.

He smiled, only for an instant, leaving her breathless with the familiarity of his touch and the idea she really wanted him to kiss her. Relaxing against him, her mind shifted to her past mistakes. "You know," she stammered, "I'm not very good with guys."

"Good, 'cause I'm not really a guy. I'm your best friend." Adjusting his hold, he lifted his chin, challenging her to deny it.

She felt the warmth of the flush crawling up her neck, not sure if he had intended to put her in her place or if his words were meant to draw her in. Smiling faintly, she gave him a pat on the chest. "Yes, you really are. And I'm so thankful that I met you."

Slipping out of his grasp, she gave him a sideways glance, fairly certain he had no intention of revealing the meaning behind his words. Allowing herself to return to the present, she looked around at the crowd, feeling a bit less tense after his caring gesture. "I think we've done all we can here."

"Agreed." He adjusted his cart, ready to take what they had and go.

Working their way towards the front, they picked up anything that looked promising, knowing what ever came up short would have to do. Standing in line, Caleb continued to touch and caress her, using his attention to distract her from the throng of people that milled about them.

When they were finally ready to pay, they purchased their items out of her account with a swipe of her card, remembering to pull cash for two rolls of coins. "That leaves me with a little over two grand, which we may or may not want to bother pulling out. It sounds like we won't be able to wait until after dark to leave town if the storm's coming before that, so we may not have time for the stop."

"Yeah," he agreed. "We'll wanna get outta here as soon as we get the car loaded. For right now, we wait for the bus, an' I'll meet you at the house, same as before. Once we get there, we'll get the news on an' find out what the official word is on this new storm."

Executing their plan, they hauled everything up the stairs a short time later, and he switched on the television while she began packing their dry goods into their new containers. While she accomplished that task, Caleb moved to the computer, performing a few searches to locate the best place for them to shop for the vehicle.

Seeing a few that interested him, he jotted down the specifics on a notepad, grumbling to himself, "I wish this were a laptop," as he shut down the machine. "That way we could take it with us." Joining her in the front room, he inquired, "Have they said anything about th' new storm?"

"Yes." Her features crinkled in disgust. "It's going to land right on us."

"What about The Ranch? You think it'll see any of it?"

"I have no idea," she replied with a shake of her head. "I don't really know where it is exactly, and I hate to speculate."

Kneeling down next to the wide screen, he outlined the area for her with an extended finger, the next time the map popped up. "This is th' general location." He gave it a light tap. "Looks like it's right on the edge. It may or may not be hit, so we'll find out when we get there, I guess. Pack all your warm stuff an' whatever the boys have so we can take it with us."

"We should try to get ahold of them again," she suggested. "If we can't reach them by phone, we should message everyone and see if someone will respond."

"Yeah." He nodded, wishing again the computer was a laptop. "Go kick the computer back on, an' I'll try some numbers."

Doing as he asked, she made her way into the smallest bedroom and watched the icons pop into place while she shoved their warmer clothes into a trash bag and tied it shut. Pulling up her uncle's profile, she noted that there hadn't been any new posts or new comments in over twenty-four hours. Going down the list, she began to grow uneasy when she realized there hadn't been any posts made by anyone in the same length of time.

"Caleb!" she called loudly. "Something's wrong!"

Hearing her disgruntled tone, he made his way into the room. "I still don' get any answers. They all ring an' go t' voicemail, an' I tried every number in my contacts." He plunked down beside her, avoiding the top bunk with his head when he did so. "Whatcha got?"

"Nothing," she replied curtly. "No one has posted *anything* since early Sunday."

"Scooch over," he commanded, not ready to accept the entire community had dropped off the face of the earth simultaneously.

Ten minutes later, he ran his fingers through his short blond hair, emitting a loud sigh of disgust. "What the hell does it mean?"

"It means something's happened," she breathed, "and we need to get there as quickly as we can."

"Well, we are," he agreed sharply, checking the time. "We need t' go. The car lot 'll be opening soon, an' we can get that done, get loaded, an' get the hell outta here."

Making their way down the stairs, she swung onto the bike behind him, gripping him as they rode. Their first stop was the bank, where he emptied his account, the clerk giving him an odd look when he withdrew almost sixteen thousand dollars in cash.

Dropping by Bailey's credit union, she did the same, and they were on their way to the dealership.

The car shopping went smoothly, and they picked out a bright yellow Jeep Wrangler, with four doors, a back seat, and a cargo area.

It only took about thirty minutes to complete the paperwork, and with Caleb's employment and credit rating, they were able to have it financed with only two thousand dollars down.

Bailey handed the salesman her wad of cash, grinning shyly at his look of surprise. "I've been saving for it," she cooed, sliding her arm around the man next to her, implying they were a couple.

Accepting her mediocre explanation, he closed the deal, handing her the keys and allowing her to roll off the lot.

She followed her assumed boyfriend back to the apartment, a satisfied grin curling her lips. Once they had arrived, they loaded the boxed goods into the cargo area and placed the jugs for the water into the back floorboard, leaving the back seat empty.

"Well," he observed, "we're not gonna fit the motorcycle back there." He paused, scratching his head. "We can fill it with other stuff if we have time for a shopping trip. An' I guess we could get a hauler for the bike if we want to take it with us."

"I think it's a good idea, but we need to hurry. The storm will be breaking any time now, and we really need to be on the road before that happens."

"Yeah," he agreed readily. "Le's get movin'."

Two hours later, they had the bike on a small trailer, attached to the hitch on the Jeep.

The water bottles had been filled, and they had the remainder of the food in the back seat, along with the new bedding that they had purchased, their winter-type clothing, and an emergency road kit they had picked up at the auto parts store.

The last things he brought down were the weapons and ammunition that he had acquired and had hidden away, including the pistol he had given to Bailey for Christmas. *We only made one trip to the gun range,* he thought with a wry grin. *She was pretty good with it, but I wish she had gotten a little more practice.*

"I think we're set," he announced as she jumped in the passenger seat next to him. "Hopefully it'll be smooth sailin' from here."

"God, I hope so," she agreed, giving her door a heavy slam and peeking over her shoulder at the back seat. "I don't really know what we'll do if it's not, but I guess we'll manage."

TWENTY-ONE

Eye of the Beholder

TAKING THE HIGHWAY HEADED WEST, the couple sat in an anxious silence until they made the turn off and headed south. At that point, the dark sky, which had been threatening them most of the day, opened up and began pouring snow down like nothing Caleb had ever seen.

"Jesus," he cursed under his breath. "Is this what it's like up in Illinois?"

"Sometimes," she breathed a soft reply. "Beautiful, isn't it?"

He barked a laugh. "If you say so!" Shaking his head, he peered through the swirling flakes, their progress having slowed to a crawl. "I guess beauty really is in the eye o' the beholder."

The girl grinned, feeling more at ease since they were on their way. "You want to try the radio? See if we can pick up a weather report?" She pulled out her phone, glancing at it to see if she still had service, which for the time being, she did.

"Sure," he agreed readily. "But keep th' volume down."

Hitting the button, she began to scan through the channels, finding several playing music but nothing that was of any use to them. With a small sigh, she switched off the device. Gazing out the window to the right, she felt amazed at how quickly the bar ditch had filled with the white powder. "Wow, this is one hell of a storm."

"Yeah," he agreed. "We'll go as far as we can, but I don't know if we'll make it all the way on this one tank o' gas."

"Pete says it's more than a tank to drive it. I'm not sure if that applies to all vehicles though. There's that store we stopped at before," she suggested. "I'm sure we could get some fuel there."

"Maybe," he half-heartedly agreed. "I'm a little leery though, especially with th' way things have been goin' in general. When you start talking about people who live off o' the beaten path, the incidents of antisocial behavior tends t' increase, an' you really get t' see the crazy side o' human nature."

"So, you're saying we may want to avoid them," she concluded.

"Yeah." He shrugged his right shoulder. "Tha's what I'm sayin'."

"Ok," she chirped. "Then I'll see if I can find out something on the weather on my phone." She whipped it out again. "And I don't know that we could get the gas out of the bike and put it in the tank, or maybe we could take the bike and get some gas to bring to the vehicle from the compound if we can get close enough."

"Maybe," he agreed, still focused on the road and only half listening. A few minutes later, he realized she had gone completely silent and glanced over at her swiftly. "Are you ok?"

"Yes, I'm ok," her voice sounded small, and she sniffed slightly. "I just found a news story about what's happening up north. Yahoo's reporting that they've got rioting all over the place, and Chicago's been burning for hours."

"Oh my God." He felt like he'd been kicked. "Have they declared martial law?"

"Yes," she spoke, barely above a whisper. "In Illinois, Wisconsin, and Ohio. But they're expecting it to go national anytime now."

"Jesus Christ." He leaned his left elbow against the glass, catching his head in his hand as it ran roughly over his hair and face before leaning on it. "Let me guess. California couldn't stand to be left out."

Her eyes shot up to glare at him. "This's no time for jokes, Caleb." But as soon as she said it, she found herself snickering. "Oakland and LA," she admitted with a tiny grin.

"See." He smiled for a moment as well. "We're gonna be ok, little bit. We jus' have t' make it to The Ranch, an' it gets better for us."

Returning to her search, she located more on the weather. "Well, when it rains, it pours. Or snows, as the case may be. We aren't going to see a break in this line for at least three days. The front goes from Florida, all the way across New Mexico. It's unreal."

"Lovely. Well, I think we're gonna pull in at the gas station an' try our luck. I'll go in an' pay for the gas, an' I'll put your pistol in my pocket, just in case. It's smaller, so it'll hide easier."

"Won't that be dangerous?" she demanded loudly. "What if they think you're trying to rob them?"

"They're not gonna see it unless there's trouble, an' there won' be no trouble unless they start it," he clarified. "Either way, I'm not stoppin' there empty-handed."

They crept along, still moving but not making good time at all. The sun had already dropped low in the sky, and the soft grey of the storm would be shifting to dark before long. Adjusting herself anxiously in her seat, Bailey dug in her bag, locating her charger and inserting it into the USB outlet in the dash, then plugging in her device.

Continuing to scour the net, she shared her next discovery. "They've announced a quarantine in Odessa. They've had almost three hundred new cases of the flu diagnosed in the last twenty-four hours and suspect hundreds more are infected." Her head popping up, a look of horror crossed her soft features in the dim glow. "You don't think we were exposed, do you?"

Frowning, "I doubt it. Why?"

"Well, I'd hate to show up out here and make everyone sick."

"That's true," he agreed with a bob of his head. "No, I don' think we were exposed. Not that I took note of, anyways. Anywhere else reporting outbreaks that severe?"

"Yeah, several, in fact. The one in Washington State has escalated, and they're under quarantine too, with public schools shut down completely. You know"—her mind shot into a tangent—"it's amazing, having the internet like we do. We can find out about everything, almost in real time. Isn't that nuts?"

"Sure is," he agreed with a scowl, not completely convinced it was a good thing. "What else?" He glanced at her again, not willing to take his eyes off the road for longer than a few seconds but glad she had something to distract her during the harrowing ride. "Any good news in there?"

"Jim Carrey's birthday is today."

He laughed out loud. "Well, I'm sure that's good news to someone."

"Yeah, I'm sure it is." She giggled with him. A few minutes later, she cursed under her breath. "Signal's gone."

"Aww, that sucks," he agreed, noticing she still fought with the device to no avail. "Well, at least now you know why th' other one quit working. You're in a dead zone."

Bailey stopped moving, her finger poised above the device. "I'd rather you didn't call it that." She grinned nervously, laying the phone over on the dash to finish charging.

"Right." He nodded. "Well, we got some valuable info while it lasted. Jim Carrey's birthday at the top of the list." He laughed again for good measure.

Riding in silence a few miles longer, a coyote dashed in front of the headlights, causing Caleb's lightning fast reflexes to hit the brake for an instant before he chastised himself and released the pressure. It was too late, and the car had slid out of control, careening into the ditch and coming to an abrupt stop.

"Well, fuck," he swore loudly, the wipers still swiping full blast while the rest of the vehicle remained still. Throwing the shifter in reverse, he tried to back out and up onto the road, but nothing happened. Slamming it back to a forward gear, he got the same result.

"Son of a bitch." He pounded the steering wheel with his fists.

Bailey twisted in her seat, laying her hand on his arm. "It's ok. We weren't hurt."

"Yeah, but we're stuck now. An' I ain't seen another vehicle in hours. No one else's stupid enough t' be out in this mess!"

"It's ok," she reassured again. "We just curl up and stay warm. We'll figure out how to get unstuck when the sun comes up."

He turned in his seat, peering into the area behind him. "Well"—he blew a loud puff of disgusted air—"we got supplies."

"Yes, we do. Cut off the engine so we don't waste the fuel. We're going to need it later," she suggested.

"Right." He switched off the ignition. "I shoulda let you drive," he mumbled, climbing over his seat and beginning to rearrange the back.

"Why?" She watched as he pushed the bags with their clothes in them between the water bottles. "I'm from up north, but I haven't driven on this stuff much. I didn't even have a car when my parents were alive. They drove me around."

"Oh," he lamented, using the sheets and comforter from the apartment to create a small nest. "Come on." He indicated the make-shift bed. "We'll curl up in here and stay warm."

Bailey's mind drifted to the hiking boots she had left at The Ranch, thinking they might have come in handy pretty soon. Working her way between the seats, she noted his prone position, the back of the longer seat behind him. "You're too tall to actually lay down," she observed. "I'm just thankful we brought the pillows and blankets."

"Yeah, an' it's ok." He helped her get the cover smoothed over the top of her. "You bend your legs, an' I'll spoon up behind you. That's it." A moment later, they were both beneath the heavy comforters, semi-comfortable with the tops of the water jugs sticking up in a few places.

Her body contorted, she groaned. "Can I face you instead?"

"Sure." He held the blanket up enough to allow her to roll over, then repositioned it behind her, with his leg lying across hers. "Better?"

"Yup." She rested her hand against his chest, her cheek pressed into it. "Yes, I like this much better."

"It kinda puts an end to the spooning," he complained in a playful tone.

"But I can see you." She cut her green orbs, which were as wide as saucers, up at him, and his smile lessened slightly. "What's wrong?"

"I'm sorry I crashed us," he breathed against her scalp. "It was a stupid move."

"Really, we're ok. We need to be patient and conserve our resources, and we'll get unstuck in the morning."

"Yeah," he agreed, giving her a squeeze. "Goodnight, Bailey."

"Goodnight, Caleb," she agreed, laying her face back against his firm muscles and breathing deeply.

Listening to her, he deduced soon after that she had drifted off to sleep. Allowing his hand to grip her hip firmly, he thought about how she had filled out, muscle-wise, since he had been working with her. *She's grown a lot tougher,* he consoled himself. *We're gonna be fine.*

His breath moving across the top of her auburn locks, he sighed deeply. *All that time and effort, an' she's not even gonna finish school.* But they had given it their best, and their friendship had grown stronger in the process. *Friends.* He hadn't had many in his lifetime, only having been surrounded by the limited number that inhabit The Ranch for the majority of it. However, the one who lay in his arms at that moment had become his best, and the thought of losing her at this point sent a shiver down his spine.

"I'm gonna take care of you, Bailey-girl," he promised her quietly into the darkness. "The best that I can." He tightened his grip as he swore his oath to her.

TWENTY-TWO

Cold Outside

BAILEY FELT cold when she awoke, noticing her breath frost in the dim light. Her chest burned when she inhaled, and she shifted slightly, stiffly pressed against the man next to her. Her hand mashed against his muscular chest, she could feel his ribs rise and fall, deducing he was still asleep.

Pushing against him, "Caleb," she called quietly to rouse him. "Caleb, it's too cold."

Sliding his hand up from her waist, along her back and into her hair at the base of her scalp, he smiled down into her upturned face. "You want I should warm you?"

"Yes," she whispered hoarsely in return, "but we can only run the engine for a few minutes at a time."

"Sure." He continued to smile, his reference lost on her innocent nature. "Gimme a sec." Gazing out into the darkness that surrounded the vehicle, it appeared to be almost completely covered in snow, which obstructed his view. "The exhaust could be blocked." He grimaced. "We really can't run it for long."

Leveraging himself over her, he left her curled in the warmth of their nest and moved into the driver's seat. Reaching up, her hand grasped his shoulder, and she scooted into the space next to him, between the seats.

"Do you hear something?" she whispered loudly, her heart pounding out of control.

Sitting still, the air coming out of his mouth and nose turned into a white cloud and hung in the air. "Coyotes," he agreed. "Like the one that put us here."

"There must be quite a few." She trembled, leaning back into the blankets. "Ok, you can start it," she gave her consent.

Once the engine had begun to heat up, he switched on the fan to warm the pocket of air surrounding them, then cut it off and made his way next to her once again. Sitting up this time, she leaned into the crook of his lap, the back of her head against his chest.

His arm resting around her, his hand spread across her belly, causing him to grin for a moment. Nuzzling the side of her head, he instructed, "Get some more sleep, little bit," and she didn't bother to disagree, being wrapped in the warmth of him putting her at ease.

The next time the girl opened her eyes, she saw pale light through the windshield ahead of her. Shifting her gaze, she could see that the windows were covered about halfway up with snow, the upper portions being bombarded with flakes. Climbing out of the blanket, she moved to her passenger seat and did her best to peer out of the narrow band of unobstructed glass.

"Hey! That's a building!" she called quite loudly, waking the man with a start.

"What?!?" He stretched and fought to sit up at the same time.

"Over there." She poked the portal with a stiff finger. "There's a house or something over there."

Twisting in the seat behind her, he looked out as well. "Hit the engine," he instructed. "Get it warm in here for a minute."

Doing as he asked, she moved to check out each of the other windows but didn't find anything else of interest. Finally able to kick the fan on, it noisily filled the space with warmer air, leaving the cold outside for the moment.

Moving to join her in the front section, he hit the wipers to see if they would flick over. The snow covering too heavy to allow it, he sighed at the discovery. "We'll dig ourselves out in a few minutes. I need something to drink first." Fighting with the blankets, he managed to free two of the smaller bottles from their plastic shrink-wrap prison. "Don't lose these," he warned her. "We're gonna wanna refill them."

"Right," she agreed. "Hauling a five-gallon jug if we have to hike won't cut it." Caleb stopped moving and shifted his eyes over at her, blinking a few times until she noticed and met his stare. "What?" she demanded flatly.

"I wadn'talking about refillin' 'em with water." He kept a straight face.

Her eyes grew wide, a hot flush shooting up to stain her cheeks from her chest when she made the connection. "Oh my God! Men...are...disgusting! And what am I supposed to do?" She pointed the narrow opening at him. "No way in hell can I pee into this little thing!" She could see the grin slowly curl his lips. "Oh, that's funny. I guess I get to hang my rear out the window in the snow."

"Naw, I'm sure there's a funnel in the emergency kit. You just cop a squat over it, an' you're home free." Tilting his bottle, he nonchalantly polished it off while trying to avoid outright laughter at her indignation.

Refreshed, the pair continued to assess and discuss their situation. Reaching in his back pocket, Caleb pulled out his own cell, as if he suddenly remembered that he had it. "Fuck," he mumbled a moment later. "This really is a dead zone. I don' have any bars either."

"Damn," she agreed with his assessment. "Ok, we might as well see if we can get a door open. The emergency kit we picked up has that fold out shovel in it, too."

"Yeah," he agreed. "It's dinky but better than nothin'. See if you can get to it for me, an' I'll either get my door open or go out the window." Looking around again, he altered his plan. "Actually your window, since the car's leanin' that way."

Rummaging in the box, she located the device and tugged it free. "We got a lot of crap in this car," she declared "If we can't figure out how to get unstuck, we don't deserve to get out of here."

Unable to get the door to budge, Caleb rolled down the passenger window, pushing the snow out of the way and sliding out. "Oh, hell yeah!" he called joyfully.

"What?"

"It's not bad out here at all. I mean, it's still comin' down, but it's only piling up here on the car. The rest o' the area's not so deep. Once we get free, we should be able t' roll ahead, no problem." Taking the short shovel from her, "I wish we had gone ahead and asked if they had any snow chains, though. I didn' really think we would need them."

"I doubt they would have had any," she reassured him. "I mean, why would they stock those in the middle of the desert?"

"True," he agreed, applying the device to the drifts surrounding their vehicle. Arriving at the back, he double-checked their connection to the trailer, hoping that his bike had survived the mishap. Half an hour later, he was ready to test their position and slid into the driver's seat. "I dug all the snow out," he huffed slightly. "Hopefully it'll give us enough traction we can start rollin', an' then I think we'll be ok."

Sure enough, as soon as they had pulled forward a little, the wheels were able to catch, and they eased back onto the road, beginning their slow trek once again. Continuing to peer across the field at the building in the distance, she thought about what Caleb had said about the other people who chose to live in the middle of nowhere. "You think they're ok over there?"

"Oh, I'm sure they are," he reassured. "We're down to a quarter of a tank. If we get down to an eighth, the indicator light'll come on, an' we may see if we can transfer some o' the gas from the bike, like you suggested."

"Ok. We shouldn't run the heater any more than we have to, either. I'm sure it'll save us at least a small amount of fuel."

"Maybe," he agreed. "Damn, we shoulda jus bought a couple o' cans an' strapped 'em onto the trailer with the bike."

"Yes, we should have." She emitted a small laugh. "Why didn't we think of that before?"

"I know, right?" He shook his head. "But you know 'bout hindsight."

"Yes, I know," she agreed more quietly. A short time later, she could see the station in the distance. "Well, at least we'll make it."

"Sure." He raised his chin towards it. "But I'm still nervous about stoppin' there." His brow furrowed, his mind turned. "They had pay at the pump, so I'm gonna try to avoid talkin' to anyone if I can. Maybe it'll take my card, even though I cleaned out the account."

The last few miles were torture, as each of their minds flashed visions of the danger that could be in store for them. With the building drawing near, he reached into the seat pocket behind her, where he had stored her pistol, and removed it, shoving the small weapon into his jacket pocket.

Eventually guiding the wheels off the road, he eased their transport beneath the canopy, next to the dispenser, and climbed out, credit card in hand. Opening the tank, he reached to insert his card in the slot, discovering that the feature had been disabled via a hammer or some other blunt object. Pursing his lips, he caught the movement at the front of the store out of the corner of his eye.

Raising his hands slowly, he offered the small group no reason to shoot him, the few brandishing shotguns and rifles, waving them slightly for effect.

"Hidey," one in a ball cap called loudly. "You need some fuel, we take it."

"Yeah." Caleb stayed cool, watching as one of them made his way around to open the passenger door, indicating for the girl to join them. "How much for a tank?" he queried, his eyes following her as she raised her own arms, stopping at the front bumper to stare at the men who outnumbered them four to one.

"What ya got fer trade?" the apparent leader of the crew demanded gruffly. Moving over to inspect the motorcycle behind their vehicle, he grinned. One of the others seemed more interested in Bailey.

Watching the group, Caleb's eyes narrowed. The one closest to his companion called out loudly, "This yur sister, dude?"

"My wife," he offered the lie without hesitation.

"Aaahhh," the noise came, moving up and down in a sing-song fashion. "Is that yur ol' man?" He pointed his weapon at her, moving a step closer.

"Yes," she agreed, not about to go against him on the issue. Her arms shook slightly, and she raised her chin, looking down her nose at him for a moment. "We have some cash," she offered, catching a wisp of hair that had blown up in her face and become hung on her knit cap.

"Cash don' mean shit 'roun' here," one of the others stated matter-of-factly. "We'll take the bike."

"The bike!" Caleb looked stricken before he realized he had no choice. "Ok, fair enough. Start up the pump, an' you can unhitch it." He reached in his pocket to hand the ball cap the key.

Bailey watched with wide green orbs, shuffling her way closer to him while he filled the tank. Over his shoulder, she could see two of the shop dwellers had disconnected the trailer and were inspecting their new toy. Starting it, one of them backed it down the incline, revving the engine a few times before he rode away to try it out despite the swirling flakes.

Cutting her eyes over at the one who had seemed interested in her, he grinned, showing her his few remaining teeth.

"Hi," he clipped, seeing her look his way.

"Hi," she answered softly, inching closer to Caleb, who slid his arm easily around her, kissing the top of her head through her cap.

A few minutes later, the reservoir had been filled, and he pulled the hose, returning the nozzle to the pump. "Thanks, fellas." He raised a hand to them and encircled her waist with his arm to guide her.

Walking her around to the passenger side, he placed her into her seat, leaning in and giving her a light, quick peck on the lips for effect.

Closing her door with a thud, he returned to his own chair, exhaling a loud gasp of relief when they were back on the road and the station had begun fading into the distance behind them.

TWENTY-THREE

Home Free

REACHING OVER, Caleb grasped her fingers, entwining them with his own. "Thank you for playin' along." He chuckled. "I thought for a second you wouldn't."

"It surprised me." She pushed her head back against the seat. "But I trust you."

"Yeah." He grinned. "When he asked if you were my sister, I got scared he wanted t' trade you for th' fuel."

"Me, too," she breathed, watching the white scenery scroll past from the corner of her eye. Her palm resting lightly against his, she felt no need to draw the appendage away. "How much further is it?"

"About fifty miles until we make the turn off," he supplied. "After that, it's a private road, an' we're home free."

Agreeing with his assessment, she relaxed further into the upholstery, closing her eyes and allowing herself to doze. Sometime later, she awakened to the shift of the car, thrown off balance when they made the turn. "Was that it?" she inquired, noticing the rough bump of the cattle guard beneath them.

"That was it." His smile widened. "I wonder if somethin'

happened to a tower an' that's why everything has gone dark out here. Maybe that's why they seem to have disappeared."

"Maybe," she speculated along with him, freeing her hand and reaching for her phone. Unplugging it, she flicked the screen open. "Still no bars. That's an ok theory, except that my old phone had no service either." She paused for a moment, studying the screen. "Where's yours?"

Extracting it from his pocket, he handed her the device, and she opened the screen. Emitting a small gasp, she confessed, "That's not it. You're back on. Should I try to reach them again?"

"Sure." He flicked his hand at her in acquiescence. "It can't hurt."

After attempting a few numbers, Bailey darkened the screen with an exaggerated sigh. "Nothing," she confessed, dropping it onto the console between them. Sufficing herself to watch the compound grow larger before them, she could feel the knots in her stomach growing in number and size, unsure what they would find when they got there.

Arriving at the large gate, she could feel her heart in her throat at the sight of the gaping pile of twisted metal. "What the hell!"

Caleb shook his head, equally as shocked by the view. "I have no idea," he commented aloud. "It looks like someone ran into it...with a bulldozer."

Following the road, they passed the first set of wind turbines, and Bailey could see the airfield beyond, hazy in the falling snow. Keeping to the blacktop, they crept forward, arriving at the diner a moment later. The glass along the front shattered, the insides had been easily destroyed and coated with ice and snow.

"Caleb, don't stop here!" she begged in a quiet voice.

"No," he agreed. "We'll have a look around before we get out."

Continuing down the path, the armory on the right stood open, more than likely cleared. The gun range beyond, he made a right onto the last path, using the cul-de-sac in front of the med center to turn around, noting that the building appeared to be unharmed, as did the gym. Back at the pavement, he pulled across, passing by the water tower and rolling slowly by the greenhouse, which stood ajar.

Making the complete loop, the buildings appeared to be in varying degrees of turmoil, windows broken randomly and doors left open. Not seeing any sign of another living thing in the blanket of frost that covered the ground, Caleb pulled up at the garage in front of the stables and killed the engine. "Come," he half whispered, reaching behind the seat to retrieve his rifle and the box of shells.

Outside, he pulled the pistol from his pocket, holding it out to her. "Here." He waived it slightly towards her, waiting for her to take it.

Her hands trembling, she grasped the cold steel. "Caleb, I—"

"Shh," he cut her off, raising a single finger to his lips. "Use your shots sparingly," he whispered, "an' stay close to me." Moving in slow motion, he led her to the stables, where they slipped in through the wide door in the end, which stood half open, careful not to touch the wood.

Inside, the dark space crushed in around them, and they stood still, waiting for their eyes to adjust to the low light. A few minutes later, they moved through the structure, discovering the stalls were empty. Exiting the far end, they moved under the canopy, and he froze in front of the barn door. "Someone's still here." He indicated the footprint smaller than his own, which had filled in with snow.

Staring at the outline, she realized it was too big to belong to her brothers and too small to be that of her uncle. Her breath frosting, she began to inhale in a deep pant, the realization that her family was missing slowly taking hold of her. Following her best friend, they crept towards the center entrance so that the rabbit cages would be on their left and the larger pens would fall to the right.

Inside, the light from the skylights above them bathed the wide room in a soft glow, the vacant stillness of the area sending chills up her spine. Reaching forward, she laid her hand lightly on his arm, dismayed that everything of value seemed to be missing, especially the people.

Hearing the sound of an engine outside, the couple scampered to the end, and he peeked out from the swinging double door, pushing against it lightly to achieve the smallest of cracks. "Fuck me. It's the guys from the station. Tha's why they let us leave."

"What do you mean?" her voice trembled.

"They let us go so they could follow us," he deduced aloud. "Stay here," he commanded. "Get in a corner, an' shoot any o' them that find you. You remember what I taught you about that, right?"

"Shoot to kill," she repeated his words from the gun range. "What if I can't?"

"Then you'll become their prisoner," he supplied. "An' they're gonna beat you...an' rape you. An' if you're lucky, they'll kill you." His eyes bore into her. "You understand?"

"Yes." She gripped his arm firmly, heart pounding against her ribs. She then released him, turning slowly to choose her hiding place.

Leaving her, he crept out the direction they came in, making his way to the end of the building, away from her haven. Moving through the stables, he planted himself with his rifle, hoping to use their empty transport as bait.

Sure enough, the group discovered the wrangler a few minutes later, exiting their own vehicle to inspect it. Taking aim, Caleb had the first one down, followed by the second in short order, before the remainder of the group ducked for cover, still unsure of his location.

He knew from their previous encounter there were at least eight of them, if they all made the journey. Somehow, he didn't think they would have left their own turf unprotected. *Of course, there could have been some still inside when they confronted us.* His thoughts churned, assessing the situation and formulating a plan.

Spying the machetes that hung on the wall next to the wide frame, he stood, collecting one and pressing his tall form into the space created by the wide wooden beams for a moment. Waiting patiently, he knew they would begin to search for him, and a few minutes later, one of them poked his head through the door.

Caleb knew the man would be blind, the light inside the stables much lower than that outside. Allowing his target to step further in, he swung the heavy blade, nearly removing his head with a single action. His body slumping to the ground, the searcher's legs gave a few violent kicks, then lay still, his blood flow slowing to a mere ooze and steaming lightly in the cold.

Standing over him, Caleb peered out the door, dimly aware that he had never actually taken a human life before. He had trained for it since he was a child, their family never secretive about their beliefs or intentions. Seeing nothing moving beyond in the swirling frost, he weaved through the structure, coming out at the covered portion of the corral. *They know we're here,* he rationalized. *The snow gives us away.*

Retracing his own steps, he crossed towards the barn, aware that the men had taken their vehicle and moved away. Deciding to leave the girl where she had hidden, he turned right and jogged to the far end of the barn, making his way around the corner and venturing down the road that lay between it and the outside wall.

Gliding through the trees, he reached the steps that would be invisible to anyone who didn't know they were there. Quickly, he scaled the structure and climbed over onto the top, which stood about three feet thick.

Panning the ground below him, he spied his targets grouped on the pavement that ran through the first collection of windmills. *Must be planning their next move,* he speculated, counting four heads. He knew he would be lucky to get two of them before they again found cover.

Looking down the scope, he identified the one that had appeared to be in charge, taking him out with a clear shot, then catching his second while he ran towards the front gate, as if he wanted to escape the compound. Standing, Caleb jogged down the wall, taking the ladder that ran directly beside the gate and following his prey towards the buildings in the center of town.

Their footprints clearly visible, he hung back, aware that one of them had gone up the steps to the Smalls' porch and probably cowered inside the dwelling. The second had gone straight down the road, his tracks headed towards the diner. *Or he's sneaking back around towards the barn.* He briefly thought of the girl.

Aware he had to deal with the man that lay before him, the blond man exhaled slowly, calming himself and preparing for the push. Moving ahead, he did his best to remain behind their parked Jeep, noting the open doors. Hunching down, he snuck up beside it, clearly able to see the marks that indicated he was on the right track.

Close to the side of the garage, he veered to the right, standing up straight behind it and slinking down the back to the far end. Moving towards the duplex and the playground that lay between it and the airstrip, he exhaled thick frost from his nose. Reaching the corner, he froze, seeing the man standing between the house and the garage, as if trying to decide what to do.

Raising his weapon, Caleb dropped him, then jogged down the path. Stepping over the man's body, he took a knee at the corner to observe the front of the diner. Seeing that nothing moved, he stood and darted across the street, taking the path that would lead him back to Bailey, when a shot rang out before him, and panic gripped his throat.

TWENTY-FOUR

Cry in the Dark

BAILEY LEFT Caleb to hunker into a corner, where the rabbit cages that remained hid her from plain sight. Struggling to calm herself, she inhaled and exhaled in a steady rhythm. Aware of every noise around her, the barn seemed eerily quiet without its normal inhabitants.

Staring straight ahead, she heard the sound of two shots, then silence. Her pulse heavy inside her throat, she waited, hearing the vehicle that had pulled in only moments before make its retreat. She could tell from the noise that it had moved to the other side of the barn and guessed that it had returned to the main road. Silently, she prayed that Caleb had not been the victim of the shots.

Squatting, her heart twisted in agony, she did not dare to move, as obviously more of the interlopers remained. Hearing more shots, she smiled, more certain that she had heard the sound of justice and that her dearest friend was settling the score. *Hopefully we get one of them alive,* she thought with the faintest of grins. *I'm sure he could tell us what happened to everyone else.*

A few minutes later, she heard the door at the front creak, and her body stiffened. She could see the toboggan-covered head moving through the wire cage before her, appearing and disappearing in the mesh as it moved slowly forward. A moment later, a voice called to her, "You might's well come out, missy. Yur ol' man's dead."

In shock, she struggled to hold her breathing in check. Hearing her ragged pants, he swung his weapon to face her, and she held her own, pointing it towards him, the barrel shaking slightly as she inched towards him. "I don't believe you," she gasped.

"Oh, it's true, honey." He grinned, and she recognized the few teeth that were exposed.

"You're the one from the store," she accused.

"Yup." He continued to smile, pleased with his prize. "You didn' really love that guy, did you?"

She stared at him, still clutching the pistol, thinking about the tall blond man who had become a huge part of her existence. She needed him almost as much as she needed air, and the thought of his passing paralyzed her. "I said I don't believe you." Fighting her anguish, she raised her arm and leveled the barrel at him.

Laughing, the stranger stepped towards her. "You ain' gonna shoot me," he speculated. "If you was, you already woulda." Pausing, he waited for her response.

"Don't move!" she called loudly, attempting to retreat but finding herself blocked by the wooden trough behind her.

He nodded, laughing as he took another giant step.

Pulling the trigger, she caught her breath at the sight of the blood spewing from the back of his head and the sound of his body falling to the ground. A moment later, she could hear a voice calling her name. "I'm in here!" she shouted, lowering her weapon and working her way past the corpse, not daring to move too close to it.

Making his way inside, Caleb caught her, wrapping his arms around her and hugging as tightly as he dared. He could feel her tremors, his eyes taking in the scene. His fingers weaved their way through her silky auburn locks, searching for her warm scalp. Sliding her cap out of the way so that his face pressed against her, "It's ok," he breathed onto the top of her head. "We got 'em all, little bit."

Overcome with emotion, the girl began to sob loudly, clinging to him with the darkness of the barn heavy around them. Allowing her to do so, he waited for her spasms to subside before he crowded her changing existence with the discomfort of their reality.

"Bailey, listen." He finally pushed her head back, searching her eyes. "Everything's gonna be ok, but we need t' move."

"I killed him," she whined, tears spilling over to streak down her face.

"Yeah." He placed his lips against her forehead. "I'm sorry, Bailey. You didn't have a choice. You know that," he stated more firmly.

Pulling herself away from him, she wiped at her streams of sorrow, only glancing at the lifeless form. "Where is everyone?" she demanded, realizing they had no prisoners and no one to interrogate but each other.

"I don't know." He shook his head slightly, aware of her muddled state.

"We need to get help." She allowed the pistol to dangle from her fingers, holding it towards him. Her mind leaping to his phone, she stepped towards their car. "I need to call the police," she stammered.

"The police?" he demanded loudly. "For what?"

"My brothers are gone," she moaned. "I need the police to help us find them."

"Bailey!" His voice loud, he shook her firmly, trying to reach through her fog of confusion. "We're in the middle o' nowhere. They are rioting all over the country, an' civilization is in turmoil. Do you really think the cops are gonna care about two lost little boys?"

She stared at him, her green eyes glowing in the dim light. A moment later, she stammered, "Caleb?"

"Yeah." He stroked her back with one hand, his other shifting to her jaw. "It's ok. We're gonna be fine." He nodded. "An' we'll do what we can t' find them. I promise."

"Hey!" another voice cut into their conversation, and Carson came bolting in from the entrance, throwing his arms around his older sibling. "How did you get here?" he screamed.

Registering the younger Cross, Bailey sniffed loudly. "Carson! Where are the boys?"

"I dunno," he whimpered, then burst into actual tears.

Taking charge, the taller male guided them both out into the drifting snow. "Come on, you two. We need to get someplace warm and get set up." Looking down at his younger brother, he continued, "Is anyone else here?"

"No." The red-headed boy sobbed. "I been alone for days. Since they took them."

"Ok, then we need t' find where we're gonna hunker down. Which building is th' least damaged, do you think?" he continued to grill the boy.

"Our house ain' so bad." He shrugged.

Taking that as a positive, Caleb loaded the pair into their vehicle and drove them around to their quarters, parking in the back next to the kitchen and the rear entrance. The three of them grabbed a few items to carry inside and gathered in the familiar space to regroup. Having a look around, he discovered that all of the windows were intact, and the front door would close. The structure seemed warm, and he asked absently, "Have you been hiding here?"

"Yes," Carson admitted, "but there's no food."

"It's ok." His brother clamped him on the shoulder. "Bring in the rest o' the boxes, an' we'll get situated here." Turning to Bailey, he continued to give commands. "We have electricity. You can cook us a meal, an' I'll gather their weapons an' Jeep, in case we need them."

Nodding, the girl set to work, finding her way to the kitchen, only to discover the stove didn't come on. Searching for the breaker box, she reset the flipped switches, returning to her task a moment later.

Carson placed the boxes on the counter and floor, then hauled in a jug of water. Discovering the smaller bottles, he opened one and chugged it, hardly taking a breath while he did so. Then, returning to his chore, he gathered the blankets and pillows, placing them on the sofa, along with the bags of clothes.

Caleb returned shortly thereafter, carrying the weapons and ammo he had collected from the dead men. "We'll have to search the buildings," he stated calmly, laying his spoils on the table. "See what we might be able t' find that's of any use t' us."

"There ain't much," Carson countered. "The cops took everything they could carry. Including the people."

"The cops?" Bailey's mouth hung open. "The police did this?"

"Yeah." He took a step back, unsure about her obvious anger. "They came with a helicopter, an'—"

"Wait," Caleb cut him off with a raised hand. "We want to hear all about it, but first things first. We need t' get the meal prepared an' nourish ourselves. We need water an' figure out where we're gonna rest. Has anyone else been here besides the cops, us, and the guys we killed?"

"No." Carson shook his red locks. "It's been just me for a couple o' days, until you got here."

"Ok, then we can feel pretty safe staying here in the house." He reached out, grasping his brother's shoulders, one in each hand. "You did good, watchin' th' place. Go spread out the blankets in the living room, an' make us some pallets so we all have a place t' sleep."

"What's wrong with the beds?" Bailey demanded.

"I want us all in the same room," he replied calmly, watching his brother move to do as he was told. He cut his eyes over at her. "I think we're safe, but who knows for how long."

"Ok." She nodded, returning to the pans and preparing the meal. A few minutes later, she noted that Carson had dragged an actual mattress down the stairs and assumed it was for her.

Finishing the food, she placed the items on the table, and the trio sat down to eat. The silence only broken by the sound of three hungry people, they consumed their first good meal in at least twenty-four hours. Watching the others, Bailey noted that Caleb kept an eye out the windows, not looking forward to any surprises.

When they had eaten, she cleared the mess, and the boys helped her wash and put the utensils away. Moving to the living area, they spread out, choosing their spots.

Caleb opted for the couch so he could see out and down the road through the legs of the water tower. Bailey stretched out on the make-shift bed that the younger Cross had prepared for her, while Carson tossed blankets across the oversized chair, his accommodations for the night.

"Now"—Caleb indicated his younger sibling with an open palm —"you can give us your story."

TWENTY-FIVE

Vengeance is Mine

CARSON STUDIED his older brother for a moment, then turned his attention to the girl. "Are you really one of us?" he demanded.

"One of you?" she breathed, as if he had punched her in the gut. "Yes, of course. I wouldn't be here if I wasn't!"

The boy didn't look very convinced, frowning beneath his flame-red hair. "There was a fight among the *menfolk* the same day the cops came. Mom said it had to do with you." He glared at the girl, then shifted it to his brother. "An' somethin' to do with you. An' 'Manda's baby. They was really pissed about that."

"'Manda had her baby?" Caleb inquired quietly.

"Yeah," his younger sibling supplied. "Only it wadn'yours."

"I know," the older Cross stated flatly. "How did you find out it wasn't mine?"

"Kathy said so." Carson turned his palms to the ceiling. "Soon as it was born, she came over to the diner, where everyone was waitin' an' eatin' lunch. After that, the *menfolk* called a meetin', only it was private, an' everybody got locked out. Even Mom an' the rest o' the wives."

"When they came out, they tied up Devon…an' they beat 'im with a long stick. Then they untied him, an' he married 'Manda."

"He married Amanda!" Bailey gasped.

Caleb chuckled. "I guess we know who the baby daddy is." His eyes flicked over at the girl. Nodding to her, he felt relieved that her faith in him had been justified. "So, when did the cops come?"

"That same day," Carson continued. "Things had calmed down after all that business over th' weddin'. Then all at once, this helicopter comes over an' flies around, real low like they're lookin' us over. Then it lands over on the airstrip."

"The sheriff gets out of it, an' some o' the *menfolk* go over t' meet him. They stand there for a long time, talkin' 'fore things get loud. I could tell Dad an' Pete was shoutin' at the guy, wavin' their hands around an' pointin' at stuff. An' the next thing we know, they's both on the ground, bein' shocked by one o' those zapper things."

"A Taser," Caleb supplied.

"Yeah." The boy shrugged his agreement. "They got that. An' some of the others got shot."

Bailey could feel the color drain from her face. "Who others, Carson? Who got shot?"

"Some o' the *menfolk*. They left their bodies layin' out on the ground, too. That's when a whole mess o' cops showed up. They went to gatherin' up people an' tyin' us up, so I hid, an' they didn' find me."

"They took all our stuff," Caleb finished for him, his clear blue eyes seething with anger.

"Yeah." The boy hunched his shoulders. "All our stuff an' all our people. 'Cept me an' the ones I buried."

"Did they get it all?" Caleb's eyes darted over at Bailey for a moment. "You know…any of the special stores?"

Carson followed his gaze. "Naw, only what they could see. I ain't touched 'em though. Too scared to go in there alone so I jus' ate what I could find. I killed a big rat in the barn yesterday, after it started to snow. It wadn'so bad."

"A rat!" Bailey exclaimed, her eyes flicking back and forth between the two males, momentarily in shock.

"O' course," Caleb praised his younger sibling. "That was good thinking. I bet you did all right."

"Ok." Bailey pushed the disgusting image aside. "What are special stores then?" she inquired calmly, not fooled by their attempt to keep her in the dark.

"We have a few things hidden." Caleb grinned. "Sounds like they didn't get it either. Pisses me off that they took the rest. What the hell gives them the right t' steal our stuff?"

Bailey shrugged. "Eminent domain, maybe?"

Running his fingers through his blond spikes, her friend grunted. "That's some shit right there. An' that applies to people, too?"

"Maybe they were arrested for trying to stop them." Bailey sighed, realizing that was only plausible for the adults. "I don't really know. I'm just guessing here. What I do know is that we need to get them back. And they better hope to God my little brothers weren't hurt in the process. I already killed one man, so I'm going to hell. What's a few more going to hurt now?"

"Jus' be careful with that kinda thinkin'," Caleb warned her softly.

"What?" Her eyes grew wide with an innocent stare.

"*Vengeance is mine, sayeth the Lord,*" he quoted for her. "Thinkin' about gettin' even with someone doesn't make for good choices."

"That may be true," she agreed with a small nod, "but they better watch their backs just the same. We'll get our people back, or there will be hell to pay, one way or another."

Caleb stared at the young woman, rocking his jaw side to side. *An' here I thought she was the meek an' quiet type.*

TWENTY-SIX

Won't Ever Be His

CALEB AWOKE to an eerie silence the next morning, one he had never heard before. Sitting up on the sofa, he glanced out the front window, staring down the road. It remained pitch black, and he thought he should be relieved, but he wasn't.

Something was missing in the small community—almost as if he should be hearing the heartbeats of the people asleep in the houses around him. Sighing into the darkness, he hunched over so that he rested more comfortably but could still see down the stretch of snow-covered pavement. A few minutes later, he became aware that Bailey's eyes were watching him in the dim light from her makeshift cot.

"Hey," he whispered to her.

"Hey, yourself," she retorted softly.

Grinning, he offered her his hand, guiding her to stretch out beside him and wrapping her in his arms beneath the blanket. Out flat on her back, his body positioned above hers, she felt awkward. "I'm not used to lying in bed with men. And yet here we are, for the second time in two days."

"This isn't a bed," he countered evenly. "An' neither was the other time."

"We're on cushions and wrapped in blankets, and it's night. Humor me." She giggled.

"Humor you?" His thumb traced her lips softly. "Do you wanna share my bed?"

Bailey studied the blue eyes above her. "I didn't say that," she whispered.

"Hmm." He nodded. "You've got playin' coy down to a science." Lifting his head, he looked towards the gate in the distance again. "I don't like this. It doesn't feel right."

"It shouldn't feel right." She caught his fingers, lacing them with hers. "Our friends are dead or missing, and our families are scattered. The world is in chaos, and there's nothing we can do about it."

"Yeah," he agreed with her assessment, "but it's more than that. I need t' check on somethin'. But we'll wait until sunrise. After that, we need t' make a plan."

"What do we do until then?" Her heart began to beat wildly inside her chest, her excitement getting the better of her as she squeezed his palm that pressed against hers.

His lips curling oddly, he removed his digits from her grasp, using them to graze her jaw. "You realize I'm not gonna touch you. Not like that," he whispered hoarsely.

"Like what?" she panted, hoping he would stop toying with her.

"You remember that day at the barn, when we heard…someone… you know…" He could play that game, too.

Bailey only stared at him, unable to say any more.

His grin grew wider. "Come on. I know you remember. I imagine you've thought a lot about that day."

The color instantly rose in her cheeks, having flooded her face from her chest moving upwards. "Ok, yes. I know that day."

"You told me you wanted it t' be perfect. Your one an' only soulmate forever." His finger traced her neck, detecting her warmth.

"I didn't say it like that," she denied.

"Doesn't matter how you said it," he breathed, his face inching closer to hers. "I know how you meant it." He froze, his air brushing against her inflamed skin. "I would never take that from you, Bailey. I want that for you—for you to have…exactly that."

Her green orbs stared at him, her body stiff with fear. "I don't understand," her voice trembled. "I thought you wanted me. All this time." She inhaled sharply. "Oh God, how stupid of me!" She reached up, grabbing his arms and chest to push him away. *I'm really ready, and he's throwing it away?*

Using the weight of his body, he forced himself across the top of her. "Stop!" he commanded slightly louder than he intended, his gaze darting over to his slumbering brother. Pausing to be sure the boy still slept, he whispered quietly, "Don't go away mad." His tender tone returned, his blue eyes bore into her. "I didn't say I didn't want you. Ok?"

She lay beneath him, her tremor easy to detect. "Please, get off of me."

"Sure." He stroked her again, fighting the temptation to kiss her. "If you promise me one thing."

"If you'll let me up, I'll promise you anything."

He smiled, aware he may have passed on his only chance to have her, and she would never be his. "It's not really a promise if you don't intend to keep it."

Bailey clenched her teeth, causing the muscles in her neck to flex. "Fine. Just tell me what you want. Please."

His blue eyes wide, Caleb could feel the pant start deep inside, his lungs taking on a will of their own, and he grew afraid he would lose his nerve. Raising his hand, his fingers slid into the edge of her hair, his palm grazing her forehead before it moved across the shiny auburn strands. With the intimate caress, he could feel her soul, her very being beneath him.

The girl stared up at him, caught in the sound of the air as it rushed in and out of his open mouth. The look on his face said it all, and she wanted nothing more than to be his. *Completely...irrevocably...his.* "I promise," she whispered. She lifted her face, and he tried to pull away, but she moved quicker, her hands looping his neck and the back of his head, her lips finding their way to his.

A moment later, he was free, tearing himself away before he did anything stupid. *Anything we might both regret.* "I'm sorry," he managed between deep gasps. "That wasn't right o' me." He sat on the couch next to her, and she worked herself into an upright position as well.

"It's ok." She grinned, unexplainable joy dancing inside her, as if a thousand butterflies had taken flight behind her breasts. "I understand."

He stared at her, puffing slightly as if his mouth refused to close. "Ok, what is it you understand?" His eyes narrowed when she made no attempt to respond. "You can stop it any time. I know you're jus' fuckin' with me now." He tried to remove the taste of her by applying the back of his arm to his lips.

"No." She giggled. "I swear that I'm not. I have this...fear, I guess you could call it, that I won't ever get that chance. Too many things are wrong in the world, and not enough of them are right. But it's ok, Caleb. I made my promise to you, and I swear on my life I will keep it." Not waiting for his reply, she stood, making her way to the bathroom, closing the door behind her.

TWENTY-SEVEN

Welcome to Lawson

CALEB FLOPPED his head back onto the top edge of the couch so that he stared at the ceiling above him. *Damn.* She obviously wanted to be with him. *Why didn't I just do it?* But he knew why, and there was no point in second-guessing his decision.

Sitting in an awkward position, he noticed the room growing lighter. Raising his head, he straightened, watching sun glint off the snow outside. His brother still sound asleep, he wondered if the boy had rested at all when he was alone. *Probably not.* Giving himself a good shake, he stood and stretched and moved to the kitchen to begin the search for breakfast.

Just as Carson said, everything in the house was gone, and the only food to be had they had brought with them. Searching through the items, he located things he thought would make a good morning meal, gathering them on the counter. A few minutes later, Bailey came out of her place of hiding and began to help.

Glancing at the girl, he noticed that her face had been washed, and she appeared calm. He also got the idea that she was ignoring him.

Taking his items, she pulled out a pan and began to prepare them.

A few minutes later she suggested quietly, "You should wake your brother so he can have some while it's hot."

Obeying her command, Caleb moved to the other room, giving the younger Cross a firm shake. Roused, the boy went to the bathroom, washing his face and then joining them at the table. The trio ate the odd collection in silence, and Caleb considered that the atmosphere could not have been more awkward if they *had* made love.

Nourishment completed, Bailey cleaned the kitchen while the boys had their showers and dressed warmly, as if to leave her behind. Discerning that was their intention, she decided to put her foot down.

"I'm coming with you," she stated firmly, pulling on her shoes.

"Not right now," the tall blond challenged. "I told you I have to check on somethin'. After that, we can make our plans from here. Jus' hang out an' wait, an' we'll be back—fifteen minutes or less."

Staring at him, her mouth hung open, her green eyes wide with bewilderment. "Don't leave me here. Look, I know you're going to look at something you don't want me to see. What is it? Their bodies? Your secret food? Just tell me, God dammit! I'm part of this place, too!" The flood of tears came in a rush, surprising the boys but startling the girl more.

Taking in her slender frame, Caleb grimaced. "Stop that. You want those things frozen to your face?"

Carson laughed loudly, pointing at the girl before his brother smacked him across the chest with an open palm. "Shut up. I get t' pick on her. You don't."

The younger boy wiped the spot roughly. "Oww. Why do you get to an' not me?"

"Because"—Caleb grinned, cutting his eyes over at her—"she's my girl."

Bailey's expression changed in an instant, picking up on his playful tone. "Your wife, you mean," she countered, tugging her jacket on and preparing to exit the structure with them.

Carson's grey eyes darted between them. "You guys're jus' jokin' about that, right?" When neither of them responded, he laughed. "I know you are."

Leaving the door cracked on the back side of the house, the trio walked through the compound, the stillness of it wearing on their nerves. Crossing the road, they arrived at the armory, which faced the Cross residence and butted up against the gym. The door stood open, and inside, the contents had been completely removed.

Walking across to the wall on the end, where the gym lay, they paused. Drawing a deep breath, Caleb puffed the warm air into his hands. "You realize you are never t' speak to anyone about anything you see today. Understand?" He turned enough that he faced her squarely, waiting as if he had all day.

"Yes, of course." She opened her palms to the ceiling, the suspense killing her. "I won't ever tell anyone," she added with a small smile while her hand flicked. "Cross my heart."

Reaching out to the slats that covered the wall, he slid his finger along one of the boards, applying pressure, and it popped up in a small section, exposing a keypad, into which he quickly punched in his code. The device made a long beep, and a large section of the partition swung away from them, exposing a staircase that went straight down into the darkness.

Turning on a flashlight she didn't know he possessed, he guided them through the dark tunnel, taking it slowly on the run of steps that measured about four foot wide, lined on both walls by brick and concrete. A handrail ran along each side, and Bailey gripping one of them for a moment, finding it to be cold through her glove, she pulled her hand away in disgust.

After about fifteen steps, they arrived at a flat area, four by four, where the staircase turned and descended again. Reaching the bottom, another wide, flat surface faced them, and this time, he simply pushed against it, and it gave way, opening into an equally dark cavern.

Stepping inside, he reached to the left, where she could hear the switches flick before the fluorescent lights began to flicker, warming up before exploding to life. Before them lay a chamber, roughly fifty feet straight across and another fifty feet from their vantage point to the far end, with fifteen feet to the closer end to the right.

The room contained four large dining tables, with ten chairs each, and a large sunken seating area in the center, shaped like a circle, forming a large pit in the middle of the floor. The outside wall of the room was lined with bookcases, all laden with reading material and textbooks. Lastly, several other chambers could be seen exiting the massive hall.

Gazing around her in awe, Bailey inhaled deeply, taking it all in. Her eyes finally making their way to the man who stood beside her, she exhaled the breath in a loud sigh.

Nodding, Caleb smiled, relief fluttering across his features. "Welcome to Lawson."

Books in the Irrevocable Series

RENDERED
RETAINED
RECOMBINED

COMPLETE BOXED SET

Flowchart

MAP OF CHARACTERS IN THE IRREVOCABLE SERIES

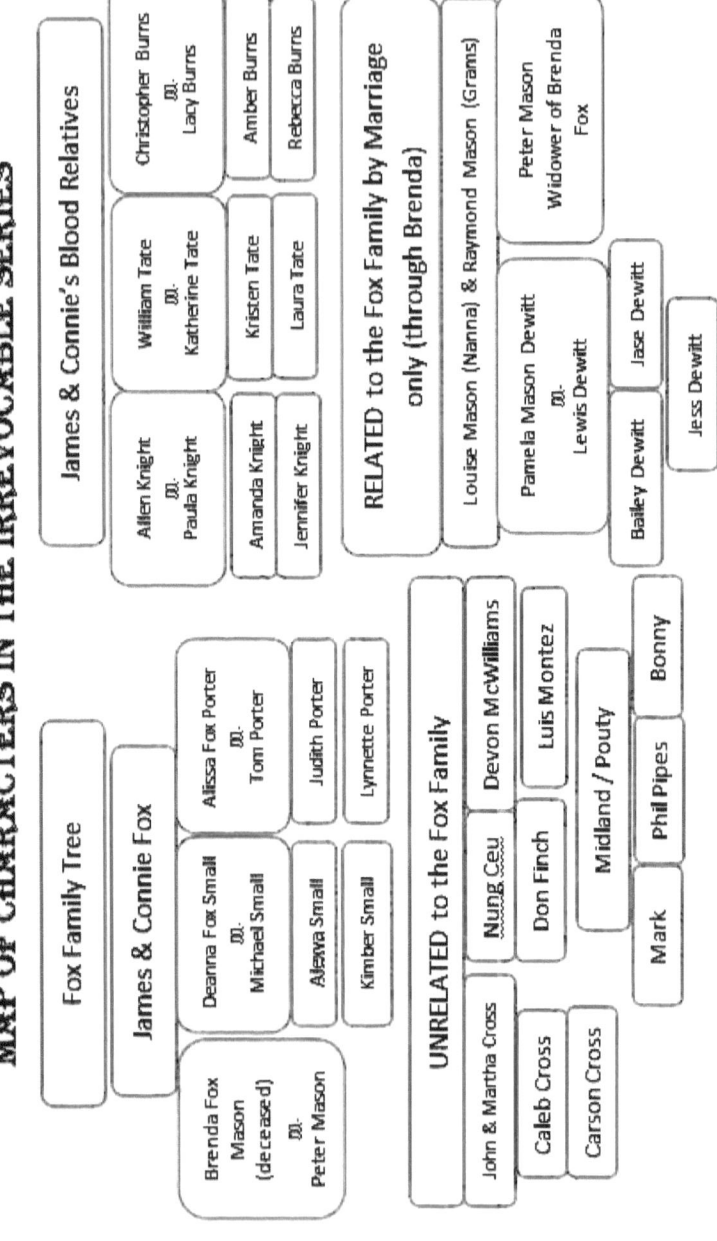

Fox Family Tree

James & Connie Fox

Brenda Fox Mason (deceased) m. Peter Mason

Deanna Fox Small m. Michael Small
- Alexxa Small
- Kimber Small

Alissa Fox Porter m. Tom Porter
- Judith Porter
- Lynnette Porter

UNRELATED to the Fox Family

John & Martha Cross
- Caleb Cross
- Carson Cross

Nung Ceu

Don Finch

Devon McWilliams

Luis Montez

Midland / Pouty

Mark

Phil Pipes

Bonny

James & Connie's Blood Relatives

Allen Knight m. Paula Knight
- Amanda Knight
- Jennifer Knight

William Tate m. Katherine Tate
- Kristen Tate
- Laura Tate

Christopher Burns m. Lacy Burns
- Amber Burns
- Rebecca Burns

RELATED to the Fox Family by Marriage only (through Brenda)

Louise Mason (Nanna) & Raymond Mason (Grams)

Pamela Mason Dewitt m. Lewis Dewitt
- Bailey Dewitt
- Jase Dewitt
- Jess Dewitt

Peter Mason Widower of Brenda Fox

Map

Map

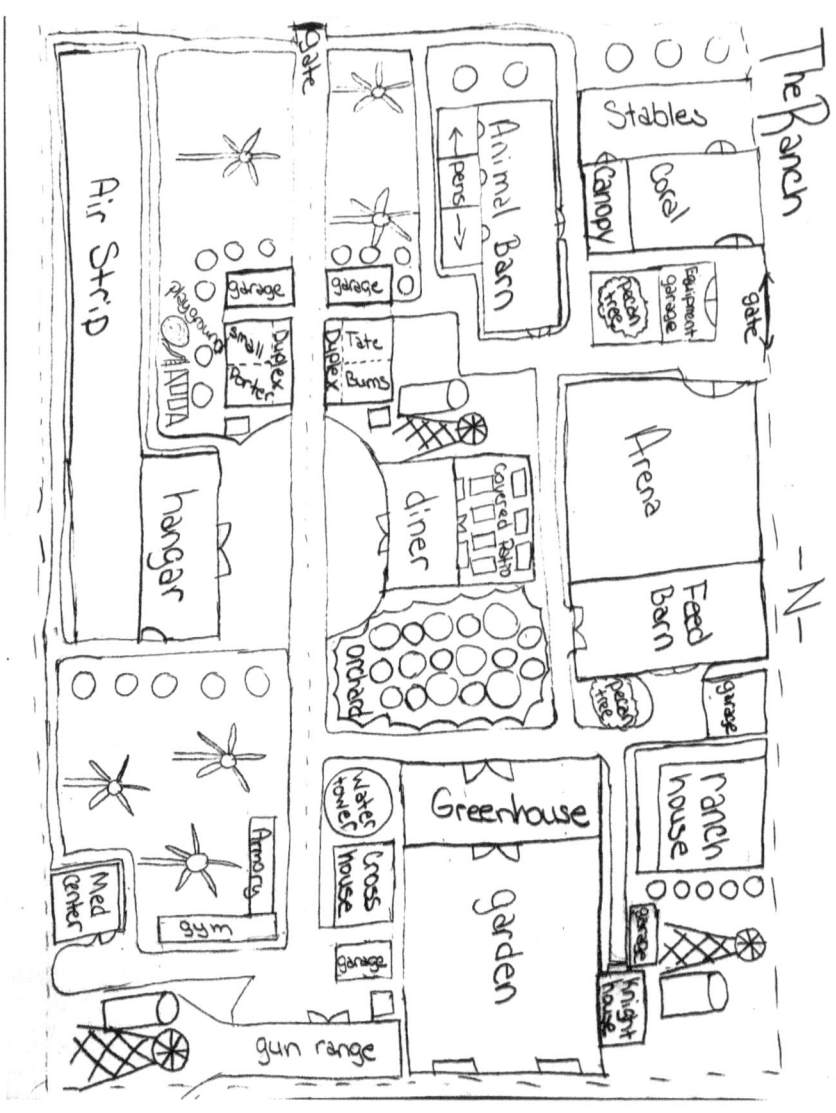

About the Author

Anyone who knows me could tell you, I am a friendly kind of person, never met a stranger and take up conversations anywhere at any time. I work hard, and my mind never seems to shut down, as I wake up often in the middle of the night with ideas pouring out and demanding to be dealt with. Of course that means much of my books were written in the middle of the night.

I grew up and still live in the great state of Texas where everything is bigger, where we have warm weather and a central location. I love my state, my town, and my family, which includes my four sons, my significant other, and many friends as well.

I have thoroughly enjoyed writing this story and hope that you will love reading it just as much. And of course, there will be many more adventures to come.

You can follow Samantha Jacobey at:
Website: www.SamJacobey.com
Facebook: https://www.facebook.com/SamJacobey
Twitter: https://twitter.com/SamJacobey
Pinterest: http://www.pinterest.com/samanthajacobey/

Also by SAMANTHA JACOBEY

http://www.amazon.com/-/e/B00GEB5LX0

A New Life Series – an epic adventure, TORI FARRELL's life IS one wild story... escaped from a biker gang and running from drug lords... used by the FBI and hoping to protect her present from her past... IT'S DARK - IT'S BRUTAL, and it's WORTH EVERY MINUTE OF IT!! (Mature read, 18+ for graphic sexual content and violence, including rape)

Summer Spirit Novella Series - no one EVER had a summer romance like this... Charlie visits another plane, parallel to our own, where Summer Angels and Dark Angels battle over the fate of man. A unique twist on an old idea that will keep you guessing; will Charlie and Clarisse ever find their HEA? (New adult)

Teach Me to Prey – in this standalone thriller, JASON TRUITT and his friends have gotten their way for years. Deceit, sex, and foul play aren't normally covered in the curriculum, but they're doing whatever it takes to get under BECKY STEWART's skin. When one of the boys turns up dead, it's a race against time to save the others; a STUNNING STORY that will get your heart racing and leave you breathless by the end... (New Adult)

The Binding (Unexpected Magic #1) - One cursed diary will change two strangers forever...Can Meri and Rider use her mother's old book to figure out why someone is after them? Or will the guilty party succeed, ripping the tome away before killing them and then slithering back into the darkness... (New Adult)

The Wicked Awakened (Unexpected Magic #2) – a Halloween novel; a five-hundred-year-old witch wants to turn SARAH MATTHEWS' body into her new home... A twisted tale involving a coven hell bent on seeing that she succeeds. Who will come out on top in this epic battle of wills? (Mature read, 18+ for graphic sexual content and violence)

Sweet Christmas Series - Life isn't always sweet, even for girls called

Candy. Candice Parker's life has never been easy. Plagued by losses and setbacks, each day is a struggle for the petite brunette and her young son. When fireman Gary enters her world, he is one mistake she refuses to make; but after tragedy strikes, she may not have a choice. (New Adult)

The Dragon of Eriden Series - Amicia Spicer led a simple life, until she discovered it had all been a lie… On her deathbed, Arely Spicer confessed to her only daughter that she had been found by, not born to her mother and father. Sad news to be certain, the idea of having a family of flesh and blood waiting to be reunited sent the young, independent woman on the adventure of a lifetime. Little did she know, a dragon's heart beat within her chest and her journey would be more perilous than she could have imagined... (New Adult)

Also from the Lavish family

The Hunter Series

Sara J. Bernhardt

http://mybook.to/HuntersTril

Jane Callahan is a reclusive, seventeen-year-old high school student dealing with the death of her beloved brother. Her home in Southern California with her mother is a constant reminder of her loss and pain. In hopes of escaping her past she moves to North Bend Oregon to live with her father, where she meets a beautiful boy named Aidan Summers.

Jane is intrigued by his looks as well as his unusual ways of attempting to get her attention. After months of uncommon conversation and frustration, an uncertain romance brews between Jane and Aidan, but Aidan has a ghastly secret that could destroy everything.

The Norn Novellas
A. Nicky Hjort
http://myBook.to/NornNovellas

The Norn Novellas are all chapters in the epic saga of the youngest and most fickle of the four Norn Sisters. The same feisty immortal creature who must escape her inherent inner darkness to learn the meaning of life.

Each story takes a classic fairytale and spins it on its head, as we learn that maybe Norse Mythology was so much more than legend. And to think, you thought you knew those old tales so well.

Meet Za and find out what really happened...

www.ingramcontent.com/pod-product-compliance
Lightning Source LLC
Chambersburg PA
CBHW022103170626
46808CB00002B/581